Roberto & Me

Roberto & Me

A Baseball Card Adventure

Dan Gutman

HARPER
An Imprint of HarperCollinsPublishers

Library of Congress Cataloging-in-Publication Data
Gutman, Dan.
    Roberto & me : a baseball card adventure / Dan Gutman. — 1st ed.
        p.   cm.
    Summary: Stosh travels back to 1969 to try to prevent the untimely
death of Roberto Clemente, a legendary baseball player and humanitarian,
but upon his return to the present, he meets his own great-grandson who
takes him into the future, and what he finds there is more shocking than
anything he has encountered in his travels to the past.
    ISBN 978-0-06-123484-2 (trade bdg.)
    ISBN 978-0-06-123485-9 (lib. bdg.)
    [1. Time travel—Fiction. 2. Baseball—Fiction. 3. Clemente, Roberto,
1934–1972—Fiction. 4. Conduct of life—Fiction. 5. Global warming—
Fiction.] I. Title. II. Title: Roberto and me.
PZ7.G9846Ro   2010   2009014267
[Fic]—dc22   CIP
                                                                    AC

Typography by Alison Klapthor
10   11   12   13   14   LP/RRDB   10   9   8   7   6   5   4   3   2   1
❖
First Edition

To Julie Krass, librarian of Deerfield
School in Westwood, Massachusetts,
who figured it out

Acknowledgments

Thanks to the following people for the kind help they gave me on this book: Warren Friss of Topps, Dave Kelly of the Library of Congress, Pat Kelly and John Horne of the National Baseball Hall of Fame, Dave Arrigo of the Pittsburgh Pirates, Jo Pure of the Haddonfield Public Library, Nina Wallace, Zach Rice, Rachel Trotta, Bob Feist, Dr. Kevin Browngoehl, Peter Blau, Richard Milner, Liza Voges, Rachel Orr, and all the folks at HarperCollins.

"*The mythic aspects of baseball usually draw on clichés of the innocent past, the nostalgia for how things were. Fields of green. Fathers and sons. But Clemente's myth arcs the other way, to the future, not the past, to what people hope they can become. His memory is kept alive as a symbol of action and passion, not of reflection and longing.*"

—David Maraniss
Clemente: The Passion and Grace of Baseball's Last Hero

Introduction

With a baseball card in my hand, I am the most powerful person in the world. With a card in my hand, I can do something the president of the United States can't do, the most intelligent genius on the planet can't do, the best athlete in the universe can't do.

I can travel through time.

—Joe Stoshack

1

It's All You

"STOSH, YOU ARE THE MAN!" BRIAN WENZEL YELLED FROM our dugout. "The man with the plan!"

I stepped up to the plate and tapped my bat against my spikes. It was the sixth inning, which is the last inning in our league. One out. Joe Koch was on first and Clay VanderMeeden was on second. A double would tie it for us. A home run would win it. I'm not a home run hitter. In a situation like this, a single would make me very happy.

I looked over at our coach, Flip Valentini, to see if maybe he wanted me to lay down a bunt to move the runners over to second and third. I figured there was a pretty good chance, because Flip knows I haven't been hitting very well lately. I struck out in the second inning, and in the fourth I hit a weak grounder back to the pitcher. If I hit into a double play right now, the game would be over.

But Flip wasn't looking at me. He was looking at the runners and touched his right arm to his left sleeve. *The steal sign.* Flip was telling Joe and Clay to attempt a double steal on the next pitch. Then he looked at me and touched his right ear. *The take sign.* He was telling me I shouldn't swing no matter what.

Okay, I get it. If I were to drop down a sacrifice bunt, we would give up an out to advance two runners into scoring position. But Joe and Clay are both pretty fast. If they pull off a double steal, we move both runners without giving up an out. So then we would have two chances to drive in the runners instead of one. Smart. Flip has been around forever. He's probably forgotten more about baseball in his life than I'll ever learn.

The pitcher looked in for his sign, and then he looked at Clay on second. He wound up and threw. Out of the corner of my eye, I saw Joe and Clay digging for second and third. The pitch was right down the middle. I probably could have hit it pretty hard. But when Flip tells me not to swing, I don't swing.

"Strike!" hollered the ump.

The catcher jumped up from his squat and fired the ball to third. Clay came sliding in with a cloud of dust. The throw was there. The third baseman only had to catch the ball and slap the tag on Clay's leg.

"Yer out!" hollered the ump.

Ouch! Two outs. Clay didn't argue the call. They had him by a foot. The catcher pointed his finger toward third as if it was a gun and blew on it. *Jerk.*

Joe advanced to second on the play.

I looked over at Flip, and he shrugged his shoulders. You win some; you lose some. Even smart strategy fails sometimes.

All I knew was that I could still tie the game. But I'd need a hit, and I hadn't had one in a while.

"C'mon, Stosh!" Flip yelled, clapping his hands. "It's all you, babe. All you."

"Drive me in, Stosh!" Joe shouted from second base.

I dug my cleats into the dirt of the batter's box. The pitcher looked in for the sign. He wheeled and delivered. It looked outside to me. I didn't swing.

"Strike!" hollered the ump.

Okay. That was borderline. Maybe it was a strike. Maybe not. Doesn't matter. Don't think about the past. Worry about the present and the future. Two strikes now. Gotta protect the plate. Swing at anything close. No way I'm gonna strike out looking.

I tried to remember all the advice people have given me over the years: *Relax. Keep your eye on the ball. Take a breath. Quick bat. Turn your hips. Bend your knees. Don't grip the bat too tightly. Take a practice swing. Focus.*

Too much to think about.

The pitcher was ready now, and so was I. He went into his windup and let it fly.

The pitch looked good, and I took a rip at it. I got a piece of the ball, but not a good piece. It went curving into foul territory down the first base line. The catcher and first baseman gave chase.

"Get out of here!" I yelled at the ball, trying to will it out of play.

The first baseman leaned against the fence and reached over into the first row of seats. It didn't look like he was going to get it, but I guess the ball was curving back, because it ended up at the top of the webbing of his glove. Part of the ball was showing. A snow cone, we call it.

Shoot! Nice catch, I had to admit.

"Three outs!" hollered the ump. "That's the ball game, fellows."

I cursed at myself and trudged back to the bench. Nobody wants to make the last out of a game. And nobody wants to make the last out on a lame pop foul.

"You'll get 'im next time, Stosh," Brian said.

What was I doing wrong? Maybe I was trying too hard. Maybe I wasn't trying hard enough. Who knew? There are so many things that can go wrong when you're hitting.

I remember reading in some book that the hardest thing to do in any sport is to hit a baseball. I mean, think about it. You're holding a round bat and you're trying to hit a round ball. That's not easy right there. Plus, a good fastball reaches the plate about a half second after the pitcher releases it. You have like two-tenths of a second to decide whether or not to swing. The ball could be coming at different speeds, from different locations. It could be a curveball. It could be out of the strike zone, making it hard to hit. Or it could be coming at your head. Even if you manage to hit the ball, if you hit it a fraction of an inch too low or too high, you're probably out. Or somebody in the field can make a great play and catch it. And sometimes you hit it right at somebody.

No wonder players who can get a hit just three times in ten at bats are considered superstars. It's a game of failure. You fail seven times out of ten and you're doing great.

I chucked my bat against the fence near our dugout in disgust.

"Hey, none of that, son!" the ump yelled at me.

I plopped down on the bench next to Coach Valentini, who was wiping his forehead with a handkerchief.

"I suck," I muttered to nobody in particular.

"You're in a slump," Flip said. "It happens to everybody, Stosh. Even the great ones—Cobb, Williams, DiMaggio, Aaron—they all had slumps. I remember this one time in 1954—"

Usually I enjoy listening to Flip tell his baseball stories about the good old days. But today, I just wasn't in the mood.

"What can I do to get out of my slump?" I asked him.

Flip has been playing and coaching baseball for something like seventy years. If anybody knew how to get out of a slump, I figured it would be Flip.

"Ah, the great mystery of life," he said. "Nothin'

5

you *can* do. Fuhgetuhboutit. You just gotta wait it out, Stosh. Believe me, the hits will come. You're too good a hitter to stay in a slump for long."

He was trying to make me feel good. I didn't want to hear it.

I was packing up my equipment when I heard a buzz in the bleachers behind our bench. I turned around to check it out. It was a troop of Girl Scouts. They were marching through the crowd with cans. I figured they were selling cookies, but then I noticed one of them carrying a sign that said SAVE THE POLAR BEARS.

"Oh, give me a break," said our third baseman, Ricky Hernandez.

"Hey, why don't you girls get a life?" said our catcher, Teddy Ronson, when the Girl Scouts got within earshot.

"Why don't you guys get a conscience?" said the girl holding the sign. "Do you realize that burning fossil fuels has warmed the atmosphere so much that Arctic sea ice is melting, making it harder for polar bears to hunt for food? In forty years, they all could be gone. Extinct."

"Boo-hoo. I'm crying," said Tommy Rose.

"Ya think that if humans were dying off, the bears would go around with cans collecting money for *us*?" said Lucas Riley.

"Hey, you girls should adopt the polar bears and turn them into pets," said Tommy.

We were all laughing. The guys started in making

cracks about the Bad News Bears, the Care Bears, Smokey the Bear, and every other kind of bear they could think of.

I had to admit that I felt the same way. I've got enough problems of my own trying to hit the ball. I can't worry about a bunch of bears.

"What are you gonna do with that money you're collecting?" I asked. "Buy freezers for the polar bears?"

All the guys laughed and gave me high fives, which made me feel good. At the same time I felt a little guilty. I've got nothing against polar bears. I just don't like fouling out with the tying run on second to end the game.

2

A Mission of Mercy

AS I PEDALED MY BIKE HOME, I MANAGED TO GET MY MIND off the game by thinking about my birthday. It was coming up, and I decided to ask for a portable video game system. I have a secondhand Game Boy that is like a thousand years old. But I saw in a magazine that Nintendo has a new system coming out that is very cool.

I hopped my bike over the edge of the driveway and wheeled it into the garage. In the kitchen, my mom was preparing dinner, still in her nurse's uniform. She works in the emergency room at Louisville Hospital. Usually she works the night shift, but today she was home early.

"Hey, Mom, I was thinking," I started, "for my birthday—"

I probably should have checked her mood before launching into the conversation.

"Mister, you're in trouble," she told me.

She didn't have to tell me I was in trouble. I knew I was in trouble because the only time my mother ever calls me "mister" is when I'm in trouble.

She handed me a piece of paper that said PROGRESS REPORT at the top. In between report cards, my school sends out progress reports to parents to let them know if their kid is screwing up or not. I don't know why they call it a progress report if they basically say you're not making much progress.

The progress report said that I was doing fine in all my classes except Spanish. There was a note that said POOR WORK and some code after that.

"I thought I was doing okay in Spanish," I said.

"If flunking is okay," my mom said, "you were right. It says that if you don't do something to bring up your grade, Joey, you're going to get an F on your next report card."

I'm a pretty decent student. Let me say that right now. But I would be the first to admit that I'm not very good in Spanish. I just don't get it. I don't see why I have to learn a foreign language, anyway.

At my school, we have to take Spanish, German, French, and Italian, each for one marking period. Then, at the end of the term, we choose one language to study the following year. I'm definitely *not* going to choose Spanish.

The next day, like it or not, I had to go talk to my teacher, Señorita Molina, to see what I could do to

9

bring up my grade. I have Spanish last period on Thursdays, so I just waited until the other kids left the class before approaching Señorita Molina.

She's an okay lady, I guess. Kids think she's kind of strange. Like, she keeps a lit candle on her desk at all times, but she never tells anybody why.

Señorita Molina can't walk. She's in a wheelchair, and the whiteboard in her classroom is lower than normal so she can write on it from a sitting position. There have been lots of times in the lunchroom when me and some other kids sit around and try to guess what happened to Señorita Molina to make her disabled. But nobody knows for sure. And nobody has the nerve to ask her. She's one of those teachers who gives you the impression she doesn't want to talk about personal stuff.

"*Buenos dias, Tito*," she said when I came over to her desk.

Tito is my Spanish name. On the first day of school, Señorita Molina said that each of us had to choose a Spanish name for ourselves. Most of the names sounded lame, but Tito sounded kind of cool, so I chose it.

"My mom got the progress report in the mail," I said.

"I was disappointed, Tito," said Señorita Molina.

"I'll try harder," I told her.

"Tell you what," she said. "You can do an extra credit project to bring up that grade."

"What sort of extra credit project?" I asked.

"Whatever you like," she said. "*Usa tu imaginación, Tito.* Use your imagination."

She looked down at her papers, so I figured she was finished with me. I was about to leave; but then I figured, what the heck? Nobody else was around. It was just the two of us. What did I have to lose?

"Señorita Molina," I said, "why do you keep a candle burning on your desk?"

She looked up at me, not with anger in her eyes but with sorrow. She paused for a moment, as if she wasn't sure she wanted to confide in me or not.

"It is for Roberto Clemente," she finally said.

Well, being a big baseball fan, I knew a thing or two about Roberto Clemente. Just about the only thing I ever read is baseball books. I've got a whole shelf of them at home. I know a lot about baseball history, both from reading and from seeing it with my own eyes.

I knew that Roberto Clemente played for the Pittsburgh Pirates, mostly in the 1960s. Rightfield. He had a great arm, and he was one of the few players to reach 3,000 hits. No more, no less. 3,000 hits exactly. He's in the Baseball Hall of Fame.

Señorita Molina reached into her drawer and pulled out a framed picture.

"I met Mr. Clemente when I was *una niñita*, a very little girl," she told me. "I grew up in Puerto Rico, and so did he."

"How did you meet him?" I asked.

"I was so young, I barely remember," Señorita

It was a photo of Roberto Clemente. He had even signed it.

Molina said. "It was toward the end of 1972. I developed an infection in my spine and had to spend the whole year at San Jorge Children's Hospital. That's in San Juan. There was a *medica mentos*—an antibiotic—that could have made the infection go away, but my family was very poor and could not afford a hundred dollars to pay for it."

"Is that why you have the wheelchair?" I asked.

"*Sí.* Yes. Anyway, Mr. Clemente visited the hospital one day. He would do that all the time. There were no photographers or reporters there. He just did it because he cared. And he was so nice. The big baseball star—sitting at the edge of my bed! He told my parents that he was going to come back in a few weeks and give me a hundred-dollar bill so I could get the antibiotic I needed to get better. But he never did."

At that point, I could see Señorita Molina's eyes were wet. It occurred to me that maybe I never should have asked her about the candle.

"Why do you think he didn't come back?" I asked.

"Because *se murio*. He died, Tito."

Señorita Molina dabbed her eyes with a tissue and told me what happened. On December 23, 1972, there was a huge earthquake in Nicaragua, which is in Central America. It just about leveled the capital city, Managua. 350 square blocks were flattened. Two hospitals were destroyed. The main fire station collapsed. 5,000 people died, and 250,000 were left homeless, with no water or electricity.

Señorita Molina told me that Roberto Clemente had played winter baseball in Nicaragua and grew to love the people there. He wanted to help. So he organized a relief effort in Puerto Rico to get food, medicine, and clothing for the survivors of the earthquake. And he personally paid for a plane to fly the supplies to Nicaragua. He even insisted on going on the plane himself to make sure the stuff got to the people who needed it.

At that point, Señorita Molina cried as she pulled a yellowed newspaper clipping out of her desk drawer and showed it to me.

Clemente, Pirates' Star, Dies in Crash Of Plane Carrying Aid to Nicaragua

Special to The New York Times

SAN JUAN, P.R., Jan. 1 — Roberto Clemente, star outfielder for the Pittsburgh Pirates, died late last night in the crash of a cargo plane carrying relief supplies to the victims of the earthquake in Managua.

Three days of national mourning for Mr. Clemente were proclaimed in his native Puerto Rico, where he was the most popular sports figure in the island's history. He is a certainty to be enshrined in Baseball's Hall of Fame. He was only the 11th man in baseball history to get 3,000 hits, and his lifetime batting average of .317 was the highest among active players.

Mr. Clemente, who was 38 years old, won the National League batting championship four times in his 18-season career, was named to the All-Star team 12 times and in 1966 was named the league's Most Valuable Player. He was also one of the finest defensive outfielders with a very strong throwing arm. He led the Pittsburgh Pirates to two world championships, in 1960 and 1971, the latter time being named the Most Valuable Player in the World Series.

Continued on Page 48, Column 8

"It was *La Noche Vieja*—New Year's Eve," Señorita Molina told me. "The plane was loaded with 40,000 pounds of cargo, more than it was supposed to carry. The pilot was sleep deprived and in danger of losing his license. The crew was unqualified. There were mechanical problems too. The plane was only *volano* . . . how do you say . . . airborne for two minutes before it crashed into the ocean. Five people died, including Mr. Clemente."

"I'm sorry," I told her. I didn't know what else to say.

"*La Noche Vieja* is one of the biggest nights of the year in Puerto Rico," she told me. "Mr. Clemente left his wife and three young sons that night to help the earthquake victims. He was not looking for publicity or fame. It was a mission of mercy. In Spanish—as you should know, Tito—the word '*clemente*' means 'merciful.'"

14

I felt like it was time for me to go. I thanked Señorita Molina for giving me the chance to bring up my grade.

But after I left the classroom, I stopped dead in my tracks in the hallway. An idea popped into my head.

I could stop it!

I could go back in time and make sure Roberto Clemente didn't get on that plane.

I could save his life.

3

Just Do It

I GUESS I NEED TO DO A LITTLE EXPLAINING. ONE DAY, WHEN I was a little kid, maybe eight or nine years old, I picked up one of my dad's baseball cards. He used to have a huge collection, and his cards were all over the house. It drove my mom crazy. In fact, that was one of the reasons they got divorced.

Anyway, I picked up this card that was on the table. It was an old card. I don't even remember who was on it. I was staring at this card, and, suddenly, I felt this strange tingling sensation in my fingertips. It was unlike anything I had ever experienced before. And as I continued to hold the card, the tingling sensation became stronger and moved up my arm. It was almost like bugs crawling over me.

I kind of freaked out, you know? So I dropped the card, and the tingling sensation stopped right away.

But I was intrigued. I started experimenting with

other baseball cards. Each time, I was a little less fearful and held on to the card for a few seconds longer.

Finally, one day I was lucky enough to stumble on a Honus Wagner T-206—the most valuable baseball card in the world—and I decided not to drop it. I didn't let go of the card. The tingling sensation moved up my arm, across my body, and down my legs, getting more and more powerful until I felt like I was vibrating from head to toe. It wasn't an unpleasant feeling. Actually, it felt kind of good.

And then, suddenly, I felt myself disappearing. It was almost as if every molecule that made up my body was being digitally deleted and emailed wirelessly to another location. Very strange.

When I opened my eyes, I wasn't in my house in Louisville, Kentucky, anymore. I was in the year 1909 . . . with Honus Wagner.

But that's a story for another day.

The point is, I discovered that I have the unique ability to travel through time with the help of a baseball card. For me, a card is like a plane ticket. It takes me to the year on the card.

Since that day, I've been on a number of trips through time. I got to meet Jackie Robinson, Babe Ruth, Satchel Paige, and a bunch of other famous players. I always bring a pack of new cards with me, because that's my ticket home, back to *my* time.

Maybe I was being a little overambitious, thinking I could travel back in time, change history, and save Roberto Clemente's life. I mean, I had tried to change history before. My coach, Flip, once told me about this guy named Ray Chapman, who played for the Cleveland Indians. He was the only guy in major-league history to die from getting hit by a pitched ball. I'd figured I would go back to 1920 and save Chapman's life. It should have been simple. But I messed up, and it didn't work. Other times I'd tried to save the reputations of Shoeless Joe Jackson and Jim Thorpe. That didn't work either. I'd even tried to prevent the assassination of Abraham Lincoln. That was a disaster.

Come to think of it, I don't think I have *ever* been successful with any of my missions. I wasn't even able to see if Babe Ruth really called his famous "called shot" home run or see how fast Satchel Paige could throw a fastball.

But those are stories for another day too. The thing is, I've got this power, this gift. Nobody else in the world has it, as far as I know.

If you could do something that nobody else in the world could do, you would want to do it, right? What a waste it would be to have a special power like that and not use it. I had to at least *try* to save Roberto Clemente's life.

How hard could it be to prevent a guy from getting on a plane that's doomed to crash? Probably not as hard as it would be to convince my mom to let me go.

You see, time travel is *dangerous* stuff. It has

been for me, anyway. The time I went back to 1919 to help Shoeless Joe Jackson, a bunch of gangsters kidnapped me, tied me to a chair, and almost shot me. Another time, I took my mother back to 1863 with me, and we landed in the middle of the Battle of Gettysburg, with bullets whizzing by our heads. *That* was interesting. So I have to be careful about bringing up new time travel trips to my mother.

I finished my homework and went downstairs. Mom was at the kitchen table, paying bills and doing some paperwork. There was music coming from the radio she keeps next to the sink.

"What is that horrible sound?" I asked.

I make fun of my mother because she listens to this awful oldies music from the sixties. The "classics," she calls them.

"That's Jimi Hendrix," Mom said. "'Purple Haze'!"

"Ugh, how can you listen to that?" I said, covering my ears. "It's not music! It's just noise."

My mom laughed, because my grandparents used to say the same thing to her when she was a little girl.

"Hendrix was a genius," my mother told me for the hundredth time. "And like a lot of geniuses, he died young. He died of a drug overdose in 1970, when he was just 27. Such a tragedy."

She gave me the perfect opening.

"Mom," I said, choosing my words carefully, "speaking of people who died young, does the name

19

Roberto Clemente mean anything to you?"

My mother knew that Clemente was a ballplayer, but that was about it. She's not a huge baseball fan. I told her a little bit about Clemente and how he died in a plane crash while trying to deliver medicine and supplies to earthquake victims in Nicaragua.

"That's so sad," she said.

"Mom, I was thinking," I said, "maybe I can do something about it. I don't have to get on the plane or anything. All I have to do is find Roberto and make sure *he* doesn't get on the plane. If I can do that, he won't die. I'll be real careful. And it will be educational. It will be . . ."

I figured I would be in for a tough battle. My mother is a little on the overprotective side. You know—I'm an only child and she's a single parent and all. If anything ever happened to me, she would be all alone.

But she surprised me. It took her about a millisecond to make up her mind.

"Do it," she said simply.

"Really?"

"*Do* it," she repeated. "Joey, do you know why I became a nurse?"

"Because you're into blood and gore and guts?" I guessed.

"No, to help people," she said. "I could have chosen a career that paid more money or would have been fewer hours. Less blood and gore and guts. But I wanted to do something good for the world. I hope that when you grow up, you'll use the skills you have to help other people in some way. You should have a cause. Everyone should. So, by all means, I approve. Go save Roberto Clemente. Just be careful."

I thought about what my mother said. I confess, when I first started traveling through time, all I really wanted to do was meet famous baseball players. It was just a joyride. But when I saw how dangerous it was, I decided to do it only if I had a real mission to accomplish. I wasn't about to risk my life just to see some guy hit a famous home run. That's what video is for. And now I had come around to thinking I would only travel through time if I could do some good, right some wrong, help somebody. And if I could save Roberto Clemente's life—well, the world would be a better place. Because if he had 40 or 50 more years to help people, he could have accomplished so much more.

"Do you want to come with me?" I asked my mom.

"It's tempting," she said, "but going back in time once was enough for me."

Now for the next part of my mission, which should be the easy part: All I had to do was get a Roberto Clemente baseball card.

4

The Great One

FLIP'S FAN CLUB IS IN A STRIP MALL ON SHELBYVILLE ROAD. It's the place to go in Louisville if you want sports cards and memorabilia. Coach Valentini opened the store after he retired. Flip is the kind of guy who can never sit around and do nothing all day. He has to be busy all the time. That's the way I want to be when I retire someday.

The bell on the door jangled when I walked in. Flip's is a tiny little place, with cards and stuff jammed all over. Flip is not what you'd call a neat freak. And I doubt that the store makes much money for him. Not many kids are serious card collectors like me. But running the store gives Flip something to do when he's not coaching our team. Baseball has always been his life.

Flip was reading the newspaper when I came in. He's really old, and it shows. The little hair he has is pure white, and some of it grows out of his ears and nose. Me and the other guys on our team always tell him that he should trim that stuff because it grosses us out, but Flip says he hardly has any hair so he's not going to cut off what he's still got left.

"Hey, Stosh," he said when I came in, "I was just readin' an article about quantum physics."

"That's funny, Flip," I said.

"No, for real," he replied. "They figured out how to teleport a photon almost 90 miles."

"What's a photon?" I asked.

"How should I know?" Flip said. "Somethin' to do with dark energy and traversable wormholes, it says here. A bunch of mumbo jumbo, if you ask me. But it says that if humans ever figure out how to travel through time, when we disappear, there'll be a rush of air into the vacuum left behind. Yeah, and it says that papers are gonna fly around, and moisture will condense out of the air into clouds."

"I better watch out," I told him. "I don't want it to rain in my living room."

Flip laughed. Besides my mom and dad, he's one of the few people who knows about my "special gift."

"What can I do fer ya today, Stosh? Or are ya just here for my scintillatin' company and good looks?"

"I'm looking for a Roberto Clemente card, Flip," I told him. "You don't have one, do you?"

"Ah," he said, "Clemente. The Great One, they used to call him. Plannin' a little trip to New Year's Eve, 1972, I'm guessing?"

"Well, it doesn't have to be that exact date," I said. "As long as I can get to Roberto before he gets on that plane that killed him. I'm gonna try to talk him out of going and save his life."

"A noble mission," Flip told me. "A tip of the hat to you, my boy. Hey, here's a trivia question about Clemente: Why did he choose the number 21 for his uniform?"

"No clue," I replied.

"Because there are 21 letters in his full name: Roberto Clemente Walker. You could look it up."

Flip pulled out one of his thick baseball books and started flipping through the pages until he found the entry for Roberto Clemente.

"Look at Clemente just as a hitter," Flip told me. "He won the National League batting title four times. *Four* times! When he died, only ten other players in history had reached 3,000 hits. He played in 14 World Series games and got a hit in each one. Nobody with more than 12 World Series games can say that. And even though Willie Mays, Mickey Mantle, and Hank Aaron were way more famous, Clemente had a higher lifetime batting average than any of 'em."

"I know he was a great hitter," I said.

"He was even better defensively," Flip told me. "He won 12 straight Gold Glove Awards."

"Okay, so the guy could play the field," I said.

"Plus, he was a 12-time All-Star," Flip continued. "He was the 1966 National League Most Valuable Player and the 1971 World Series MVP, and he led the Pirates to two World Championships: in 1960 and 1971. Stosh, Clemente may have been the best all-around player in the game since Honus Wagner. He was also on the Pirates, of course."

I had no idea how great he was.

"Did you ever see him play?" I asked.

"Oh, yeah," Flip said, "plenty of times. I used to drive an hour and a half to Crosley Field in Cincinnati just to see him when the Pirates came to play the Reds. Late sixties, early seventies. But the thing with Clemente was this, Stosh: He was more than just statistics. It wasn't just numbers with the guy.

He played with a passion and intensity that nobody else had. I mean, there was somethin' almost . . . *royal* about him."

"What do you mean?" I asked.

"It's hard to put into words," he said. "You'd have to see it with your own eyes. Oh, yeah, I guess you *will* see it with your own eyes, won't ya?"

"Hopefully," I said. "That is, if you have a Clemente card."

Flip closed the book and started rooting around the store. He had to look in every drawer, cabinet, and file. Fortunately, there weren't any other customers around.

"Hmmm, this is interesting," Flip said as he leafed through a dog-eared file. "Did you know that seven major-league players died in plane crashes?"

Flip loves this baseball trivia stuff. I think he'd be happy if he just spent the whole day learning more trivia. I glanced at the clock on the wall. Soon I would have to be heading home for dinner.

"There was Clemente, of course," Flip continued, "and Thurman Munson, the Yankee catcher. His plane crashed in 1979. Cory Lidle, also with the Yankees, in 2006. Ken Hubbs, the second baseman of the Cubs, in 1964. Two guys died in 1956: Charlie Peete of the Cardinals and Tom Gastall of the Orioles. I remember them. And way back in 1925, the Cincinnati pitcher Marvin Goodwin died in a small plane crash. Well, I guess it had to be a small plane. They didn't have any big planes back then. I mean, the

Wright brothers only flew in their airplane in, what, 1903 or something?"

"So, do you think you might have a Clemente card?" I asked, trying to get Flip back on the subject.

"Hey, look at this, Stosh," Flip said excitedly. "Two of these guys were teammates! Clemente and Munson both played winter ball in Puerto Rico for the San Juan Senators one year. And they both died in plane crashes. Ain't that somethin'?"

It was something, but it wasn't something that would help me get a Roberto Clemente card. Flip and I just about turned the store upside down. He even looked in his safe, where he keeps his more valuable cards. No Clemente. It was almost as if Flip had a card for every player in the history of baseball *except for* Roberto Clemente.

He did come across a newspaper clipping about the plane crash that killed Clemente and said I could have it. I stuck it in my backpack. If I ever did find Clemente, I would be able to show him the clipping and hopefully talk him out of getting on the plane.

"Gee, I'm sorry, Stosh," Flip finally said. "It looks like I can't help you on this one after all."

"It's okay, Flip."

Well, we tried, anyway. Maybe I could find a Clemente card somewhere else. They aren't that rare. I'd just have to keep my eyes open.

5

The Card

eBay! OF COURSE!

As I rode my bike home from Flip's, I figured I'd see if I could find a Roberto Clemente card on eBay. I get a lot of cool stuff that way. One time I got a 1951 Bobby Thomson card on eBay for 11 cents. Sweet!

When I got on the computer, there was an email from my dad:

STILL COMING OVER TODAY AT 5?

Shoot! I forgot! Mom was working until midnight, and I was supposed to have dinner with my dad. I looked at the clock. Quarter to five. eBay would have to wait. I rushed back out the door and rode my bike over to Dad's place.

My dad lives in a little apartment on the other side of Louisville. I see him once or twice a week. It's not any big "custody" arrangement. We just kind of worked it out together.

Sometimes I wish I didn't have to go see my father. But then, sometimes I wish I didn't have to see my mom. They're parents, right? I bet sometimes they'd rather not see me either.

When I was little, my dad taught me how to play ball, and he got me into card collecting too. But a while back, he was involved in a car crash that left him paralyzed. So playing ball is out. We pretty much watch TV, eat pizza, and play video games together. Stuff he can do. It's okay. He loves video games almost as much as he loves baseball.

"What's the word on the street, Butch?" my dad asked when I came to the door. He always calls me Butch.

We covered the usual ground—school, Mom, girls, and stuff like that—until we got around to the thing we talk about the most: baseball. He told me that his boyhood hero was Thurman Munson, who was a catcher for the Yankees in the seventies. I remembered that Munson was one of those seven players who died in plane crashes. My dad had no idea that Clemente and Munson were teammates for a season in Puerto Rico. I like telling him something about baseball that he doesn't know.

"Did you ever see Roberto Clemente play?" I asked.

It seems like when you mention Clemente to grown-ups, they go on and on about how great he was or what a humanitarian he was. But not my dad.

"Oh, yeah, I saw him play a lot when I was a little kid," he told me. "I *hated* Clemente."

"Why?" I asked.

"'Cause I'm a Yankee fan," he replied.

Dad told me that one of his first memories was watching the Yankees play the Pirates in the 1960 World Series. Mickey Mantle and Roger Maris were on the Yankees back then, and the Yanks were favored to wipe the floor with the Pirates. But after six games, the two teams were all tied up. The winner of Game 7 would be the World Champion.

"It was the bottom of the eighth," my dad told me. "The Yankees were ahead, 7–5. It was looking good. There were two outs and two on when Clemente came up."

"And he hit a homer?" I asked.

"Nah," Dad said, "he hit this weak grounder between the pitcher and first base. Shoulda been an easy third out. But Clemente beat it out. The *next* guy hit a homer, and Pittsburgh went ahead, 9–7."

"Was that how it ended?" I asked.

"Nope," Dad continued. "The Yankees scored two runs in the top of the ninth to tie the game. But Bill Mazeroski led off the bottom of the ninth for the Pirates and hit a solo homer to end it. I'll tell you, that broke a lot of hearts in New York. The Yankees outscored the Pirates 55 to 27, but they lost the Series."

"It's not fair to blame that on Clemente," I said. "The pitcher or the first baseman should have made the play on him to end the inning. If you were gonna hate anybody, it should have been Mazeroski. He was the guy who hit the home run to win it."

"Oh, I hated him too," Dad said. "Hey, what did I know? I was a kid. I wasn't gonna blame my own team for losing."

"Clemente was a great player, Dad."

"I know, I know," my father said. "Wait a minute. Don't tell me. Let me guess. You're gonna go back in time and save Clemente, aren't you? You're gonna try to talk him out of getting on that plane."

"How did you know?"

"If I could do what you can do, that's what I would do," Dad said. "It's a no-brainer."

"I just have one problem," I told my dad. "I don't have a Roberto Clemente card. Flip thought he might have one, but he couldn't find it."

My dad wrinkled up his forehead for a moment, and then he snapped his fingers.

"I think I have one," he said.

"Really?"

My dad laughed, then wheeled himself into his bedroom, where he keeps the stuff he collects. My dad sold most of his valuable baseball cards a while ago and switched over to collecting autographed baseballs. But he kept a shoe box full of cards he didn't think anybody would buy.

The value of a baseball card depends partly on its condition. A card that has marks or creases isn't worth nearly as much as the same card in mint condition. Dad pulled a shoe box out of his closet that was labeled POOR.

"It must be in here," he said, flipping through the cards in the box. "I remember it."

"It's okay, Dad," I told him. "I should be able to find one on eBay."

"Aha!" he said as he pulled out a card.

Well, it was a Clemente card, all right. I could make out the CLE and the TE. The rest was hard to read because the card was filled with holes.

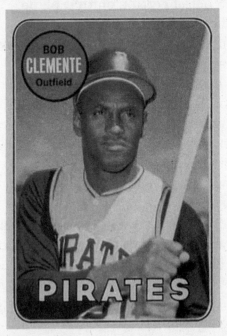

The Roberto Clemente card, before it was destroyed. Note the first name. As recently as the sixties, some Americans were still uncomfortable with Spanish names.

"What happened to it?" I asked.

"Me and my friends used it as a dartboard," my father said. "After that World Series, we really hated the Pirates."

"You messed up Clemente good," I told him.

"You should've seen what we did to Mazeroski," he said.

I didn't touch the card. If it really did work and I held it in my hand, I knew what would happen. I would get that tingling sensation in my fingertips. It would move up my arm and across my body, and the next thing I knew I would be in the year . . .

Actually, I didn't know where I would be. The Clemente card was so beat up, you couldn't even see the year on the back of it. But it didn't matter. If the card was printed any year before Clemente died, I would be able to warn him not to get on the plane.

"Do you think a card in this condition will still work?" I asked.

"Beats me," Dad said. "You're the one who has the power. Give it a shot. Keep the card. It's worth pennies. Happy birthday."

We both laughed as he carefully slid the junky card into a plastic holder.

I looked at the Clemente card closely. It may not be worth more than a few pennies in the baseball card market. But it could be worth a lot more. If I could convince Roberto Clemente not to get on that plane, he might still be alive today. I stashed the card in my backpack.

"Hey, speaking of birthday presents . . ." my dad said as he pulled a wrapped package out of his closet.

My dad hasn't worked since his accident, and he doesn't have a lot of money. His presents are usually stuff he picks up at the dollar store. I wasn't expecting much when I tore off the wrapping paper. So I was totally blown away when I saw that my present was the new Nintendo portable video game system.

"Dad!" I exclaimed. "Where'd you get the money for this?"

"Your mother chipped in on it," he replied. "It's from both of us."

I thanked him about a million times. After we had some pizza and tried out the video game system, I figured it was time to leave. My dad gets tired early, and my mom doesn't like me riding my bike home late at night.

"Hey, I got a brainstorm," Dad said as I picked up my stuff to go. "As long as you're going back in time to see Clemente, how about doing your old man a little favor while you're there?"

Uh-oh. I was afraid he was going to ask me to do something. He usually does. My dad is always cooking up some get-rich-quick scheme for me to pull off for him. Like, he'll give me money to deposit in the bank fifty years ago so he can collect the interest. Or he'll assign me to buy up baseball cards in the past so he can sell them at today's prices. It's so annoying.

"Dad, we talked about this," I said. "I'm not gonna

do some borderline illegal thing to make money. Forget about it."

"No, no, nothin' like that," Dad said. "All I want you to do is stop Clemente from getting that cheap infield hit in the 1960 World Series."

"Dad!"

"You could rewrite baseball history, Butch!" he exclaimed. "You could win the World Series for the Yankees!"

I didn't like the idea. It sounded wrong. How could I even do that, anyway? And if I was going to change history, it would have to be for a more important reason.

"Haven't the Yankees won the World Series *enough* times?" I asked.

"Ah, I guess you're right," Dad said with a sigh. "But what about this? You said Clemente and Thurman Munson were teammates one year, right? And they both died in plane crashes. Well, while you're talking Clemente out of getting on his plane, how about telling him to talk Munson out of getting on *his* plane?"

"Dad . . ."

"Think of it as saving two birds with one stone," he said. "Nothin' wrong with that, is there?"

My father looked at the portable video game system that he had just given me. Then he looked at me again.

"I'll see what I can do," I told him.

That's what my mom always says to me when she

doesn't want to make any promises. *I'll see what I can do.*

"Fair enough," Dad said, reaching up to hug me. "Oh, one last thing before you go. Remember how you said your only problem was that you didn't have a Clemente card?"

"Yeah."

"Well, I think you might have another problem," Dad said. "You're gonna have a tough time convincing Clemente not to get on that plane."

"Why?"

"Because Roberto Clemente didn't speak English."

6

Going ... Going ... Gone!

OKAY, SO ROBERTO CLEMENTE WAS FROM PUERTO RICO, AND he didn't speak English. Big deal. I really didn't think the language barrier would be that much of a problem. I mean, how hard could it be to say "Don't get on the plane!" in Spanish? If worst came to worst, I could always use sign language. It's not hard to pantomime a plane crashing into the ocean.

Of course, if I was lucky enough that my dad's messed-up baseball card actually worked and I was able to get to Roberto Clemente, it wouldn't hurt to know a little Spanish. I would want to have a conversation with him. Can you imagine if some strange kid walked up to you from out of nowhere and just said, "Don't get on the plane! Don't get on the plane!" You'd think he was crazy.

I went home and spent the rest of the night reading my *Introduction to Spanish* textbook from school.

I memorized all the numbers, greetings, and common phrases. I learned which words were masculine and which were feminine. I learned all the possessive adjectives and pronouns. I was obsessed.

In case of emergency, I practiced saying *Estoy enfermo. Necesito ayuda.* (I am sick. I need help.) I don't think I ever worked so hard preparing for a test at school. Señorita Molina would have been proud.

Just after midnight, there was a soft knock on my door. My mom had come back from working at the hospital, and she wanted to say good night.

"You're studying Spanish?" she asked. "In the middle of the night? On the weekend? Are you feeling okay, Joey?"

"I want to be able to talk with Roberto," I told her.

"So you're already on a first-name basis with him?" she said with a laugh. "Is tonight the night?"

"Yeah," I said. "Dad gave me a Clemente card. He gave me the video game system too. Thanks, Mom! It's really cool."

I opened my backpack and showed her the Nintendo.

"Wait a minute," she said. "You're not going to bring that along, are you?"

"Sure," I told her. "Why not? I thought I might have a little time, and I could play some games."

"Joey, what if somebody sees it?" my mother said. "There were no video games back in those days! People won't know what to make of it. Maybe they'll think it's a bomb or something. They might think you're a terrorist!"

"Mom, will you relax?" I said. "There were no terrorists back in those days either."

My mother rolled her eyes the way she does.

"All right," she said. "Let me pack you some lunch to take with you."

"Mom, I don't want to bring lunch."

"Joey, you're going to get hungry!"

"I'll get something to eat while I'm *there*!" I insisted.

Mom rolled her eyes again.

"So, you'll take a video game with you, but you won't take lunch?" she said. "That makes a lot of sense."

"No lunch, Mom!"

My mother sighed, which means I won the argument. She must have been pretty tired, because she usually fights a lot harder than that. There were times when she talked me into taking an *umbrella* back in time with me in case it rained.

"Hey, listen to this," I said as she kissed my forehead. *"¡No subas el avion, Roberto!"*

"What does that mean?" she asked.

"It means, 'Don't get on the plane, Roberto!'"

"That's what you spent the whole night learning?" she asked.

"No," I told her. "I learned a lot of other stuff too. Like *¿Donde esta el correo?* That means 'Where is the post office?'"

"That should come in handy, in case you need to mail a letter in the past," my mother joked. "You just be careful, okay? I know how dangerous it can be."

"I will."

"You're doing a good thing, Joey. A very good thing. I'm proud of you."

She kissed me again and closed the door behind her as she left.

It was quiet in my room. I put on a pair of jeans, my old sneakers, and a T-shirt that didn't have any writing on it. I wasn't sure what year I would end up in, but I wanted to blend in. If I showed up 40 years ago wearing a T-shirt that said something like AMERICAN IDOL or BRITNEY SPEARS on it, people might be suspicious.

Not that I own those T-shirts, mind you.

I went to my desk drawer and took out a fresh pack of baseball cards. These would serve as my ticket back home when I was ready to return to my own time. I carefully slipped the pack into one of the zippered pockets on my backpack.

I took the messed-up Clemente card out of its plastic sleeve. It was time to see whether or not a card in such poor condition would still be able to take me back in time.

I flipped off the light and sat on the bed. My bedroom was totally dark except for a sliver of white under the door. I closed my eyes and concentrated.

* * *

Nothing happened.

I didn't panic. Usually, nothing ever happens for a few minutes.

My eyes still closed, I focused my mind on the past. It was hard. Most times I know the specific year I'm traveling to, so I can concentrate on that year. This time, the year on the card had been obliterated. I would just have to go wherever the card took me. Go with the flow.

Clemente was a rookie in 1955. I knew that. He played his last game in 1972. Eighteen years. A lot can happen in that time. I had to be prepared for anything.

That's what I was thinking when the faintest tingling sensation tickled my fingertips.

Aha! The card works!

The feeling was buzzy, like a vibrating string on a guitar. I resisted the urge to drop the card. The tingling grew stronger, and then it started to move. First across my hand and then up my arm. I nodded my head pleasantly. Soon there would be no turning back.

I thought about what Flip had said. Something about quantum physics and wormholes. There was supposed to be a rush of air around the room after my body left it. Papers were supposed to blow around. I wondered if any of that stuff would actually happen. My room was pretty much a mess, anyway. Who would even know if papers blew around?

The tingling sensation was moving across my

chest, and soon I could feel it on the other side of my body. My legs were getting numb. I knew it wouldn't be long. My whole body felt lighter, as if I had suddenly lost fifty pounds. Maybe I did. Maybe that's what happens when you—

There were no more thoughts to be had. I just vanished.

Peace and Love

BEFORE I EVEN OPENED MY EYES, MY BRAIN WAS BEING pounded by an avalanche of sound. It was an awful, eardrum-rattling noise—almost like a jet taking off. Or landing. Or, more likely, crashing. It was a shrieking, screaming sound, but not a human voice. It was more like a distorted air-raid siren or a wounded animal crying to be put out of its misery. People say that the sound of fingernails on a chalkboard is horrible. This was even worse. I covered my ears, but it was no use. It was so loud I could hear it through my skull.

Maybe I'm in the middle of Roberto Clemente's plane crash, I thought. I was afraid to open my eyes.

And then, in the middle of all the noise, I recognized a tune. I knew that song. It was . . . it was "The Star-Spangled Banner"!

I opened my eyes.

I was outdoors, and there were people crowded

around me on all sides. There were people everywhere. I mean *everywhere*. They were almost all teenagers, and they were dressed in tie-dyed shirts, sandals, jeans, and headbands. It was hard to tell the girls from the boys, because almost everybody had long hair. It took a moment or two before I realized who they were.

Hippies!

For Halloween one year, I dressed up as a hippie, with my dad's old bell-bottom jeans and a wig. People thought it was a riot. I won the contest that year at school for having the best costume.

I didn't know where I had landed, but I knew when—the sixties.

The guy next to me wasn't wearing a shirt, and he had a big red peace sign painted on his chest. His eyes were closed, and he was dancing. He wasn't dancing with anybody. He was just swaying back and forth to this strange music. He had long, stringy hair; and it looked like he hadn't washed it in a long time.

"What is that noise?" I shouted into his ear.

"That's Hendrix, man," he said without opening his eyes. "Can you dig it?"

"Jimi Hendrix?" I said. "My mother loves him."

"Your mom is groovy, man," the guy said, and then he went back into his own little world.

Somehow, some way, I had landed in the middle of a Jimi Hendrix concert! If only my mother could see *this*! I stood on my tiptoes to get a better look. There was a huge speaker system mounted on giant scaffolds on either side of the stage. I have been to a few concerts, and they usually have a giant video screen so the people in the back can see what's going on. Not here. I squinted until I could make out the figures on the stage.

There was a guy sitting behind a big bongo drum. There was a regular drummer too, and a bass player. But none of those guys were playing. The only one who was playing was Jimi Hendrix.

Somehow I had landed in the middle of a Jimi Hendrix concert.

I was standing pretty far back, but I could see that he was wearing a red headband and a white shirt with fringe all over it. He must have been left-handed, because he held his white guitar the opposite way most people do.

He wasn't singing the words to "The Star Span-gled Banner." He was just playing it, with the fringe on his shirt flying all over as he whipped around his guitar and tortured the whammy bar. He never looked at the guitar. Sometimes he would lean his head back and open his mouth wide as he played. All the people around me were jumping up and down, going crazy. Nobody had ever played "The Star-Spangled Ban-ner" like *this* before.

Finally, after what seemed like a half hour, he finished the song and went right into "Purple Haze" without pausing. I knew that song, because my mom is always playing it at home.

I looked around. The sun was low in the sky. It must have been early morning. I couldn't figure out why there would be a concert so early in the day.

"Excuse me," I asked an African-American guy beside me. "This probably sounds like a silly ques-tion, but . . . what year is it?"

"You don't even know what year it is?" he replied. "That is *soooo* groovy! It's 1969. This is Woodstock, man!"

Woodstock!?

I had heard about Woodstock. My mother told me about it. It was a big outdoor music festival in New York that had performers like Hendrix, Janis Joplin, The Who, and my mom's favorite band, Creedence Clearwater Revival.

How did I end up at Woodstock? I asked myself.

The baseball card was supposed to take me to Roberto Clemente. Something must have blown me off course. Or maybe because the card was damaged, it didn't work as well as a card in mint condition would have.

Or maybe . . . could Roberto Clemente be at Woodstock? There were thousands of people spread all across this field. How would I be able to find Clemente even if he was here?

It's never easy. I wish just *once* I could travel through time and land right next to the player instead of having to go find him. Just once.

I'm not a huge music lover, to tell you the truth. I listen to the radio and watch VH1 with my mom sometimes. But most of the groups my friends like seem to be lame interchangeable boy bands and teenybopper girls who pretty much all sound the same. I didn't so much like the sound that Jimi Hendrix was making; but I had to admit, it was *different*.

That didn't mean I had to stand there listening to it. If Roberto Clemente was here, I would have to go find him.

"Excuse me," I yelled into the ear of a girl with frizzy blond hair, "do you know if Roberto Clemente is here?"

"What band is he in?" she replied. "Santana?"

She was useless. I asked somebody else, a guy wearing a cowboy hat and holding a flute in his hand.

"You mean Roberto Clemente the baseball player?" he said. "Man, I don't know. Just groove on the music, brother. Hendrix is a genius."

Huh! That's what my mother said too. Hendrix is a genius. I remembered she'd said what a tragedy it was that he died so young of a drug overdose in 1970. If this was 1969, Jimi Hendrix would be dead within a year.

That's when it hit me. There would be plenty of time to talk to Roberto Clemente. He won't die until 1972. While I was here in 1969, I could save Jimi Hendrix's life too!

Wait a minute. Who was I kidding? There were thousands of people between me and the stage. There would be no way for me to get anywhere near Jimi Hendrix. And even if I could, what would I say to him: "Just say no to drugs, Jimi"? If he was addicted, he wasn't about to stop taking drugs just because some strange kid told him they would kill him. He would laugh at me. What a dumb idea.

Hendrix finished the song he was playing and got a standing ovation. He must have been the final act of the Woodstock Festival, because as soon as he was done, all the hippies started gathering up their stuff. People began making their way out from the stage area. Suddenly, there was a narrow open path between me and the stage.

Hendrix was still up there, unplugging his guitar and chatting with his drummer. I thought for a second or two and made a snap decision. I had to give it a try. If I could pull it off, my mother would be so happy.

"Jimi!" I shouted as I pushed my way forward. "Mr. Hendrix! I need to tell you something!"

The hippies looked at me like I was crazy, but I didn't care. When you're trying to save somebody's life, you can't worry about what people think. I was about 30 yards from the stage when somebody started shouting.

"Hey! That kid is trying to get at Jimi!"

"No!" I yelled. "I'm just trying to save his life!"

"The kid is crazy!" someone else shouted.

A bunch of hippies started chasing me as I got closer to the stage.

"Jimi!" I yelled. "You're gonna die!"

"That kid must be high on something!" somebody hollered. "He's gonna kill Jimi! Stop him!"

For a moment—when I was about ten yards from the stage—I saw Jimi look at me. Then, the next thing I knew, a bunch of hippies grabbed me and threw me to the ground in front of the stage.

"Hey, knock it off!" I yelled as they started kicking and punching me. "I thought you people were all about peace and love!"

That's when somebody picked up a big peace sign and hit me over the head with it.

Sunrise

I DON'T KNOW HOW LONG I WAS OUT. PROBABLY ONLY A FEW minutes. When I came to, I staggered away, thankful those peaceniks hadn't killed me. What had I been thinking? Trying to save Jimi Hendrix from himself was probably the stupidest idea I ever came up with.

Suddenly, a guy with stringy blond hair walked over to me and stuck his face in front of mine.

"Hey, man," he said, "if life is a grapefruit, then what's a cantaloupe?"

"How should I know?" I said, pushing the guy away.

I cleared my head. I had to get back to the reason why I came here in the first place. Roberto Clemente. He wasn't at Woodstock. He wasn't anywhere *near* Woodstock. Something had gone terribly wrong. Something *always* goes wrong. Time travel is simply not an exact science.

Think, I told myself. It was hot out. It was baseball season. Roberto Clemente had to be playing ball somewhere. The question was, where?

The only thing I could do was follow the hippies as they started to pack up their stuff and make their way toward the exits. The field was a huge mess. There was mud and garbage everywhere. It must have rained a lot during the festival. People left behind tons of soggy clothes and blankets.

Some people were in no rush to leave. They were hanging around, sleeping, doing yoga exercises, or tending campfires made of burning garbage. A few were running around with no clothes on. It looked like one of those movies where an atomic bomb went off and a small group of human survivors were left to live off the land.

I spotted a newspaper on the ground, and I picked it up.

"All the News That's Fit to Print"

The New York Times

CXVIII..No. 40,749   NEW YORK, MONDAY, AUGUST 18, 1969

Okay, I knew *when* it was. Obviously, it was too late to help the Yankees win the 1960 World Series. My dad would have to deal with that. But it wasn't too late to help Roberto Clemente. He would be alive until December 31, 1972.

I flipped through the paper until I found the sports section.

Pitching Chart

FOR GAMES OF MONDAY, AUG. 18
Starting time (EDT) follows capitalized home team

NATIONAL LEAGUE

Club	Pitcher
Pirates	Moose (L)
REDS, 8:05	Arrigo (L)

(Only game scheduled)

Okay. The Pittsburgh Pirates were playing the Cincinnati Reds tonight. At 8:05. The Reds were the home team. So Roberto Clemente must be in Cincinnati.

That's where I had to go.

Getting a huge crowd of people out of a large field at the same time isn't easy. Some of the hippies had cars; but they weren't going anywhere, because the road was one huge traffic jam. Other people had bikes, motorcycles, or roller skates. Many were on foot.

Lots of kids were looking to catch a ride with somebody else who was heading in the same direction. People were holding up hand-lettered signs: NEW YORK CITY. FLORIDA. CHICAGO. And so on. One guy held up a sign that simply read ANYWHERE USA.

Then I spotted a small sign that said CINCY on it.

It was held by a pretty girl in a flowered dress. She had long, straight brown hair; a white headband; and a string of beads around her neck. She didn't look much older than me. I wondered why her parents would let her come all the way to New York by herself.

"Do you live in Cincinnati?" I asked her.

"Yeah," she replied. "You?"

"No, but I need to get there tonight."

"What's the rush?" she asked me.

"It's a long story," I told her. I didn't feel like going into all the details unless I really had to.

"What's your name?" she asked.

"Joe Stoshack," I said. "But you can call me Stosh. Everybody does."

"You look kinda straight, Stosh," she said.

"Straight?" I said. "Would it be better if I was crooked?"

She laughed, and then I realized what she meant. I didn't look like a hippie. I didn't have bell bottoms, flowers, love beads, or any of that other hippie gear.

"I guess I am," I admitted.

"That's cool," she said. "You're doing your own thing. Different strokes for different folks. My name is Sunrise."

Sunrise? I'd never heard of anybody named Sunrise.

"Is that your real name?" I asked.

"No," she said, giggling.

"What's your real name?"

"I hate my name!" she said.

"It must be pretty horrible," I said, "What is it, Barbara Hitler or something?"

She giggled again. She had a nice smile.

"It's Sarah Simpson," she said.

"Ugh! Disgusting!" I said. "No wonder you changed it. How could anybody go through life with a name like Sarah Simpson?"

She knew I was teasing her, and she hit me playfully with her CINCY sign.

"I like Sunrise better," she said. "It means a new day, y'know? Whatever mistakes you made yesterday are forgotten. You get to start all over again. That's what I'm trying to do."

"Well, I think Sarah Simpson is a perfectly nice name," I told her. "But I'll call you Sunrise if you want."

She giggled again and took my hand.

Let me admit something right now. I've never had a girlfriend. I've never been out on a date with a girl. I've certainly never kissed a girl. Usually, in school, when I have to talk to a girl, I'm totally tongue-tied and make an idiot of myself. But I felt completely comfortable with this girl. I had known Sarah "Sunrise" Simpson for about 30 seconds, and I was already in love. She told me she was 14, and it didn't seem to bother her that I was a year younger.

"Cincinnati!" we yelled as we walked past a long line of cars heading for the main road. "Anybody going to Cincinnati?"

Sunrise and I walked about a mile down the road. We were looking for Ohio license plates. There were cars from just about every *other* state, even Alaska. I didn't mind it so much though, because Sunrise was holding my hand.

We came upon a Volkswagen van with California plates. It had peace signs and flowers painted all over it. A hippie guy and girl were tying some stuff on to the roof of the van. I was going to pass them by, but Sunrise asked them if they were driving cross-country.

"San Francisco," the guy replied. "We gotta get there by Friday."

"Could you drop us off in Cincinnati?" Sunrise asked. "It's on the way."

The guy and his girlfriend stopped what they were doing and looked me up and down. I made a halfhearted peace sign with my fingers, hoping that might help me pass the hippie test.

"What are you, the fuzz?" the girl asked.

"Huh?" I said.

"Are you a cop?" asked the guy.

"A *cop*?" I said, laughing. "I'm 13 years old!"

"Then what are you doing here, man?" he asked.

"You wouldn't believe me if I told you," I said.

"Try us," they both replied.

I looked at Sunrise, and she nodded encouragingly.

When in doubt, tell the truth. That's what Coach Valentini says.

"Okay, here goes," I told them, taking a deep breath. "The truth is, I live in the twenty-first century. I can travel through time with baseball cards, and I used a 1969 card to get here."

The three of them stared at me for a long time.

"So, in other words," the guy said, "you're saying you, like, come from the future?"

"That's right."

"Stosh, are you putting us on?" said Sunrise.

"No," I told her. "I'm telling you the absolute truth. I swear on my mother's grave."

They all looked at me some more, like they didn't exactly know what to make of me. Then, finally, all three of them said, "Far-out!" They probably thought I was kidding.

"No, I mean it!" I said. "I really *am* from the future."

"Groovy," the girl said. "I can dig that."

"We're *all* from the future," said her boyfriend. "The future of our soul."

"Here, I'll prove it to you," I said as I swung my backpack off my shoulder and pulled open the zipper. "I bet you've never seen one of *these* before."

I took out my Nintendo. They gathered around me to look over my shoulder as I turned it on. It must have looked like a little TV to them.

"You can control what's happening on the screen?" Sunrise asked.

"Sure."

"Can I try?" the guy asked.

I handed him the Nintendo to play with. He got killed almost instantly because he didn't know what to do. I showed him how to move the little joystick.

"Where can I get one of these?" he asked.

"It's future technology," I explained. "You don't have it yet. But if you give me and Sunrise a ride, you can play with it all the way to Cincinnati."

He stuck out his hand and shook mine.

"The future is exactly where we're heading," he said. "Hop in."

9

A Long, Strange Trip

SUNRISE AND I PILED INTO THE BACK OF THE VAN. THE TWO hippies got in the front. They introduced themselves as Peter and Wendy, which was easy for me to remember because of *Peter Pan*.

Wendy got behind the wheel so Peter could play with my Nintendo. It took a while to maneuver around the other cars, but eventually we were away from the Woodstock madness and driving on a country road. Wendy pulled into the first gas station she came to, and Peter hopped out to pump the gas.

"Hey," he called to me through the window, "you got any bread, man?"

"Bread?" I asked. "Why, do you want to feed some birds or something?"

Sunrise broke up laughing and punched me in my shoulder.

"No man, *bread*!" Peter said. "Dollars. Pesos.

Spare change. Dig? Gas costs money, you know. We're running on empty."

Sunrise opened a little fringed purse she had and gave Peter a five-dollar bill. It seemed kind of cheap to me. After all, we would be driving hundreds of miles to Cincinnati. But I had forgotten to bring any money with me, so I was in no position to judge.

Peter finished filling the tank and went to pay the attendant. When he came back, he handed Sunrise four quarters.

"Your change," he said.

"She gets a dollar back from a five-dollar bill?" I asked, amazed. "How much was the gas?"

"35 cents a gallon!" Peter said. "That's highway robbery, man. It's 30 cents in Frisco."

Gas for 30 cents a gallon! My mom told me she has paid more than four *dollars* a gallon! For a minute, I wondered if there might be a way to bring some 1969 gas back home with me.

Soon we pulled onto a highway and were making good time. We rolled down the windows, and everybody's hair was blowing in the wind. Everybody's but mine, of course, because I didn't have enough hair to blow. Wendy turned on the radio, and there was Jimi Hendrix, singing "Purple Haze" again. The three of them all said how great Woodstock had been despite the rain, the mud, the crowds, and the garbage. I asked Peter and Wendy why they had to get to California by Friday.

"We're going to an antiwar rally in San Francisco," Peter said.

Antiwar. I had to think for a second. 1969. War. Oh, yeah. Vietnam.

"Why don't you two join us?" Wendy asked.

"I gotta get to Cincinnati," I said.

"Me, too," Sunrise said with a sigh. "I ran away from home."

"How come?" we all asked her.

"My parents," she said. "Screaming at me all the time. They hate my clothes, my music, my friends. Me."

"Your parents don't hate you," I told her.

It was probably the wrong thing to say. I didn't know her parents. For all I knew, they *did* hate her.

In any case, Sunrise clearly didn't want to talk about it. She just closed her eyes and shook her head, like nobody would ever understand her situation at home.

"How did you get to Woodstock?" I asked her.

"Hitched," she said.

My mother told me that she hitchhiked a few times when she was younger but said I shouldn't do it because you never know what kind of psycho might pick you up. Of course, hitching a ride on a baseball card can be pretty dangerous too.

Peter had been absorbed with my Nintendo but stopped to ask how I got to Woodstock.

"Did you beam yourself over, like on *Star Trek*?" he asked. "Beam me up to Woodstock, Scotty!"

The girls laughed. I had no idea that *Star Trek* had been around so long. It bothered me a little that Peter was teasing me, but I couldn't blame him. If somebody walked up to me and said they were from another century, it would be hard to take them seriously.

I pulled out my Clemente card and passed it around. Peter said he was a baseball fan and seemed genuinely interested in the card.

"It says in the newspaper that the Pirates are playing in Cincinnati tonight," I told them. "I need to talk to Roberto Clemente."

"About what?" Sunrise asked.

"Well, this might sound strange," I said, "but Clemente is going to die in a plane crash on December 31, 1972. Believe me, it's true. So I need to convince him not to get on that plane."

"You are blowing my mind, man," Peter said. "That's three years from now."

"If he's going to die in 1972," Wendy asked, "what are you doing here *now*? Why didn't you just go talk to him to 1972?"

"I didn't have a 1972 card," I told them. "I always go to the year on the card. My dad gave me this one. I didn't even know it was a '69 until I got here."

Nobody said anything for a few minutes. It seemed like they were trying to absorb what I had said. Maybe they thought I was crazy, or on drugs or something.

It was Peter who finally broke the silence. He put

down the Nintendo like it didn't matter to him anymore.

"Y'know, I like baseball too," he said quietly. "I'm a Mets fan. They stink, I know. Last place in '62, '63, '64, '65, and '67. Next-to-last place in '66 and '68. But listen, man, there are other things in life that are more important than baseball."

"Like what?" I asked him.

"Like ending the war!" he said, turning around to face me.

"Peter, don't get started," Wendy told him. "He's too young to understand."

"Do you know that the Constitution says that only Congress has the power to declare war?" Peter asked me. "And they never did! So tell me why 16,000 American kids were killed in Vietnam last year?"

"16,000?" Sunrise said. "Are you kidding?"

"No!" Peter said. "Look it up. I did."

"He always does this," Wendy told us.

"16,000 guys died, most of 'em under 21 years old!" Peter continued. "The whole war is a lie, y'know! North Vietnam didn't attack us. They're no threat to us. Does anybody even know why we're fighting them?"

"Because they're Communists?" Sunrise asked.

"So what?" Peter shouted. "It's just a different form of government. The Vietnamese aren't hurting anybody. Let 'em be Commies if they wanna be Commies!"

"Peter could get drafted into the army any day,"

Wendy explained. "If that happens, they'll probably send him to Vietnam. So we're fighting to end the war."

"It's not just about *me*!" Peter said passionately. "The whole world is exploding before our eyes, man! They shot Martin Luther King and Bobby Kennedy last year. And did you hear about that guy Charles Manson who went nuts and murdered a bunch of people last week? It's insane! We have discrimination against blacks, women, and gays. People are starving, homeless, can't afford to go to a doctor when they're sick. And what's the government spending billions of dollars on? Sending astronauts to the *moon*!"

"Peter, please calm down," Wendy said.

"Did you see that on TV a few weeks ago?" Peter continued. "Neil Armstrong stands on the moon and says it's a giant leap for mankind. I'll tell you what would be a giant leap for mankind—"

"Enough already!" Wendy shouted. "You're bumming me out, man!"

Peter managed to calm himself down, but he wasn't finished.

"All I'm saying is, we've got infinite possibilities right here on *this* planet, man. We don't need to go to the moon. Our generation is gonna change everything. We're gonna end the war. We're gonna get Nixon impeached. Just you wait and see. Peace and love aren't just slogans, man. It's gonna be a revolution. You two should come with us to San Francisco and be part of it."

Peter handed my baseball card back to me and said, "Or you can go watch Roberto Clemente hit a ball with a stick."

We all fell silent. Peter picked up the Nintendo again and started fiddling with it. I wasn't about to go to California for an antiwar rally. But maybe he had a point. Maybe it was selfish of me to devote my energy to saving the life of one baseball player when there were so many bigger problems in the world.

I had never taken hippies seriously before. It had never occurred to me that they were anything more than silly cartoon characters who said "Groovy" all the time and walked around with peace signs, flowers, and funny clothes. To me and my friends, they were a joke, a Halloween costume.

As I was thinking about all these things, I must have dozed off, because the next thing I knew, Wendy was shaking me awake.

"Rise and shine!"

I don't know how long I slept. It had to have been a long time, because it was dark out. Peter was in the driver's seat now, so they must have made a stop somewhere. Sunrise was still asleep, her head resting on my shoulder. It felt nice.

The van pulled to a stop.

"Where are we?" Sunrise asked, stretching.

"At a rest stop outside Cincinnati," Peter said. "We've been on the road for 11 hours."

We used the restrooms, and I asked Peter if he

would be able to drop me off at Crosley Field, where the Cincinnati Reds played. He said he didn't know where it was.

"Do you have a GPS?" I asked.

"A what?"

"Forget it."

We piled back into the van, and Sunrise was able to direct us to Crosley Field, which was only about a mile from her house.

"Can we drive you home?" Wendy asked Sunrise.

"I'm not sure I'm ready to face my parents yet," she said. "Can I hang with you a while, Stosh? Until I get my courage up?"

"Sure," I said.

I saw the big CROSLEY sign, and we pulled over in front of the ballpark. Peter and Wendy got out of the van to say good-bye.

"Last chance," Peter said. "You can still come with us to Frisco."

I shook my head. "Thanks, anyway," I said.

Peter and Wendy hugged both of us. They had been incredibly nice, driving us all the way to Cincinnati.

"Hey, man, I gotta ask you," Peter said, "if you've really seen the future, what's gonna happen? Did we change the world? Will the war end? Did all our protesting make a difference?"

I had been expecting him to ask that question. I wasn't sure how to answer it. Of course the world changed since 1969. A lot. But I'm no genius. I didn't know what caused the changes. Maybe hippies like Peter and Wendy were a part of it. Or maybe the changes would have taken place no matter what they did. Who really knows for sure?

"The war is going to end," I finally told them. "President Nixon is going to resign. The women's movement and gay rights movement are going to really take off. And America is going to elect a black president in 2008."

"No way!" Peter said. "Far-out!"

Peter and Wendy were ecstatic, jumping up and down and marveling at how their generation was actually going to make a difference and change the world for the better.

I went to give Peter a high five and he went to give me a low five. We met somewhere in the middle.

"I bet after this the government will never get away with starting a senseless, undeclared war against some country that was no threat to us," Peter said. "No way America is gonna make *that* mistake again, huh?"

"Uh . . ." I said, "listen, I gotta go find Roberto Clemente."

"Peace, man," Peter said, giving me a bear hug.

"Hey, Stosh, I want to give you something," Wendy told me. She climbed in the van and came back out with a string of love beads and a headband. Wendy put the beads around my neck while Sunrise adjusted the headband.

"There," Wendy said. "Now you look like one of us."

I thanked them, and Sunrise took my hand. We were walking away from the van when Peter rolled down the window.

"Hey, one more thing," he called out. "If you really know the future, who's gonna win the World Series this year?"

The 1969 World Series. I tried to remember my baseball history. Oh, yeah. That was a famous one.

"The Miracle Mets," I told him. "They're gonna beat Baltimore in five games."

"The *Mets*?" Peter said, bursting out in laughter. "You gotta be kidding me! I mean, I can believe Nixon resigning. I can believe there will be a black president. But the Mets winning the World Series? You must be joking! *Ha-ha-ha-ha-ha-ha-ha-ha!*"

I could still hear him cackling as the van pulled away.

10

Who's on First?

SUNRISE AND I WALKED AROUND THE PERIMETER OF CROSLEY Field, looking for an open ticket booth. It occurred to me that this was sort of like a date. I was going on my first real date with a girl!

There was crowd noise coming from inside the ballpark. The game must have already begun. The first few ticket booths we walked past were already closed.

"What's the future like?" Sunrise suddenly asked me. "Do you have, like, a jet pack and stuff?"

"A *jet pack*?" I said. "What's a jet pack?"

"You know, one of those things you strap to your back," Sunrise said. "It's like a backpack with a jet engine in it, and flames shoot out the bottom so you can go flying around. I saw one in a science-fiction movie."

"No, I don't have one of those," I said.

I told Sunrise about some of the cool stuff that we *do* have in the twenty-first century, like big-screen, high-definition plasma TVs, DVDs, IMAX movies, iPods, cell phones, Google, Facebook, texting, and IMing. None of them seemed to impress her very much.

"How about a flying car?" she asked. "Does your family have one of those?"

"Uh, no," I admitted.

We finally found an open ticket window. A sign said box seats were $3.50 and general admission was $1.50. Man, stuff was cheap in 1969! Sunrise pulled out a few bills and asked for two general admission tickets. The guy in the ticket booth sneered at us, I guess because of our headbands and love beads.

"They're already in the third inning, y'know," he grumbled.

"What's the score?" I asked him.

"Nothin' nothin'."

"Well, then, we didn't miss anything," said Sunrise cheerfully.

Clearly, this girl did not know much about baseball. As soon as we were inside the ballpark, my nose was assaulted by the smell of hot dogs and roasted peanuts. It had been hours since I ate anything, and I wished I had taken my mom up on her offer to pack me a lunch. When Sunrise asked if I wanted a hot dog, I quickly accepted.

"Hippies," the vendor muttered as he handed us the dogs.

We found some decent seats in the upper level, about halfway down the first base line. I scanned the field as I always do when I visit a ballpark for the first time. Crosley looked small to me, even smaller than Fenway Park in Boston. I doubted that it could hold even 30,000 people. It looked a little different from most stadiums too. Instead of a warning track around the outfield, there was a steep incline in front of the fence. I'd never seen anything like that before.

"Now batting for Pittsburgh . . ." said the public address announcer, ". . . the centerfielder . . . Matty Alou!"

Matty Alou came out of the dugout. He was wearing an orange helmet and a black sweatshirt under his uniform.

"Booooooooooooo!" yelled the Cincinnati fans.

"Why are they booing that guy?" asked Sunrise.

"Because he plays for Pittsburgh," I told her.

"That's not very nice," she said.

Matty Alou took strike one. He was a short guy, a left-handed batter.

"You really don't know a lot about baseball, do you?" I asked Sunrise.

"Sure I do!" she insisted. "The guy who hits the ball is the hitter, and the guy who throws the ball is the . . . thrower. Right?"

I slapped my forehead. This girl had a lot to learn.

Alou took ball one. One and one.

Sunrise admitted that she had never played baseball in her life, had never been to a game, and never even watched one on TV. I told her that she had a deprived childhood. No wonder she hated her parents.

Matty Alou swung and missed the next pitch. One and two.

"So, how do you score a goal?" she asked. "I mean, a point."

"It's not a goal *or* a point," I told her. "It's a *run*. Are you new to this country or something?"

"Okay, a run," she said. "Same difference."

I explained that Alou would score a run if he advanced all the way around from home to first to second to third and back to home again.

"So all he wants to do is get back to where he is right now?" Sunrise said. "That seems pointless."

Alou slapped a single up the middle and made a wide turn at first base.

"Why did he run to *that* base?" Sunrise asked me.

"Because you're supposed to," I told her. "You run to first base."

"What if he wants to run to third base instead?"

"Why would he want to do that?" I asked her.

"For the novelty of it," Sunrise replied.

"Well, he can't," I told her.

"Why not?"

"Because they've been running to first base for a hundred years!" I said. "That's the rule."

Sunrise sighed and told me that rules are made to be broken.

"Now batting for Pittsburgh . . ." said the public

address announcer, ". . . the third baseman . . . Jose Pagan!"

"Boooooooooooooo!" yelled the Cincinnati fans.

"More booing," said Sunrise, shaking her head.

On the first pitch to Pagan, Alou took off from first, made a mad dash, and slid headfirst into second base. The Cincinnati catcher whipped the ball to second and threw him out.

"Ooh, that guy tripped and fell down!" Sunrise yelled excitedly.

"He didn't fall down!" I told her. "He slid into second base!"

The Cincinnati fans erupted into cheers when the umpire signaled that Alou was out.

"What happened?" asked Sunrise as Alou walked dejectedly back to the Pirate dugout.

"They caught him trying to steal second base," I told her.

"Is he going to get in trouble?"

I tried to explain the fundamentals of baseball to Sunrise, but she didn't quite grasp them. It was like me trying to learn Spanish.

"In baseball," I explained, "the number three is very important. "There are three outs to an inning. Three strikes and you're out. There are three bases. There are nine innings, which is three squared, and also nine players on the field."

"Okay," Sunrise said. "I think I'm starting to get it."

When Pagan took the next pitch out of the strike zone, I told Sunrise it was a ball.

"What's a ball?" she asked.

"That pitch," I said. "It was a ball."

"Well, of *course* it was a ball," she said, looking at me like I was a total idiot. "What else could it possibly be?"

"No, you don't understand," I explained. "A pitch that's out of the strike zone is a ball. Unless you swing at it."

"So if you swing at it, it's not a ball anymore?"

"Now you're catching on," I said.

"I take it back. I don't get it," said Sunrise. "This is a very confusing game!"

I was just glad I didn't have to explain the infield fly rule to her. Pagan walked on four pitches.

"How come that guy is running to first?" Sunrise asked. "He didn't even hit the ball."

"The pitcher walked him," I said.

"So why doesn't he *walk* to first?"

I tried to explain to Sunrise that there was now a force play at second base, so Pagan had to run on a ground ball.

"What if he doesn't want to run?" she asked.

"He has to," I told her.

"Well, that doesn't seem very nice," she said.

"Now batting for Pittsburgh . . ." said the public address announcer, ". . . the left fielder . . . Willie Stargell!"

I had heard of Stargell. He was a great left-handed power hitter. They called him Pops. He's in the Baseball Hall of Fame.

As Stargell stepped up to the plate, I noticed number 21 step out of the Pirate dugout.

"Look! That's him," I said, pointing toward the on-deck circle.

"Who?" Sunrise asked.

"Roberto Clemente."

We were pretty far away. I squinted to see Clemente.

"Why does he have to kneel in that circle?" Sunrise asked. "Is he being punished?"

"It's called the on-deck circle," I told her. "He's on deck."

"Like, on a boat?" she asked.

Willie Stargell took ball one and ball two, but I couldn't take my eyes off Clemente. He was kneeling, with three bats leaning against his thigh. One by one, he carefully picked them up as if they were fine china and wiped them off with a rag. Then he hefted each bat before deciding which one he felt like using.

I barely noticed when Willie Stargell sliced a wicked line drive in the gap between left and centerfield. Jose Pagan, the runner on first base, got a good jump. The ball took a tricky hop off the wall; and by the time the Reds got it in, Pagan was digging for the plate. The Cincinnati shortstop took the relay and rifled a throw home. It was close, but the catcher slapped the tag on Pagan just before his foot touched the plate. The fans roared their approval. Stargell pulled into second with a double. Sunrise probably had no idea what was happening, but she got into the spirit and clapped her hands excitedly.

"Now batting for Pittsburgh..." the public address announcer said, ". . . the rightfielder . . . Roberto Clemente!"

11

The Wild Colt

CLEMENTE WAS LIKE A DOT TO MY EYES AS I STRAINED TO see him from the upper deck. I wanted to get a better look at him.

"Hey," I said to Sunrise, "let's sneak down to the box seats!"

"Is that legal?" she asked.

"It's like jaywalking," I told her.

I grabbed her hand and hustled her down the steps until we reached the lower boxes. There were a few security guards posted in the middle; but they were old guys and it didn't look like they were paying much attention. I scanned the crowd, looking for empty seats close to the field.

"I'm afraid we're going to get caught," Sunrise said as I pulled her along.

"Just act casual," I whispered. "Pretend you belong here."

Crosley Field was about half full—or half empty, depending on how you look at it. There were plenty of open seats, but most of them were in the upper deck. Finally, I spotted a few seats in the third row, near first base. We rushed over there.

"What if the people who have these seats show up?" Sunrise asked.

"They won't," I said, pulling her down into the seat next to mine. "It's the third inning. If they're not here by now, they're not coming."

Fortunately, Clemente was not one of those guys who rushed up to home plate. So we didn't miss a thing. When Sunrise and I sat down, he was still on his way to home plate, walking slowly, deliberately, like an old man. If I was the pitcher, I would be impatient. I glanced at Willie Stargell, the runner on second.

Once he was in the batter's box, Clemente wasn't anywhere near being ready to hit. First he rotated his head and neck from side to side and then twisted it back like he was doing exercises. He didn't look like he was very comfortable.

Clemente held one arm up to let the umpire know he still wasn't ready. The ump called time. Clemente scraped at the dirt in the batter's box with his toe until he had it just the way he liked it. Finally, when he got into his stance, the pitcher stepped off the rubber. The umpire called time again.

**He was deep in the batter's box. It didn't look like
he could possibly reach a pitch on the outside corner.**

"What's taking them so long?" Sunrise asked me.

"They're playing head games," I told her. "It's like poker."

Clemente positioned himself very deep in the batter's box, as far back as you could be without crossing the chalk line. It didn't look like he could possibly reach a pitch on the outside corner, even though his bat appeared to be longer than a regular bat. Also, Clemente's bat had no knob at the end. It was like one of those old-time bats with a thick handle and large barrel.

He was not a big man. The catcher and umpire

were both taller than him. He held his hands back
and low, near his waist. Stargell took a lead off second base.

The pitcher finally decided he was ready and
looked in for his sign. He delivered the first pitch, and
Clemente took it for a called strike. It looked like he
had no intention of swinging no matter what. He was
checking the timing, trying to figure out the pitcher.

The two of them fidgeted around some more, and
the next pitch came in. It looked high to me, but
Clemente liked this one better. I recalled reading
somewhere that he was known as a "bad ball hitter."

Clemente took his stride forward impossibly early
but somehow managed to keep his bat cocked until
the last possible instant. His front leg was off the
ground as he lunged at the ball. He didn't have a
classically perfect swing like Joe DiMaggio or Ted
Williams. It looked like he was throwing the bat at
the ball.

It was a violent, furious swing, and it missed. Clemente spun around and grabbed his batting helmet
so it wouldn't fall off his head. Strike two.

A few fans on the third-base side began chanting.
At first I couldn't tell what they were saying. Then I
figured it out.

"¡Arriba! ¡Arriba! ¡Arriba! ¡Arriba!"

That was on my Spanish vocab quiz just last week.
It literally means "upstairs," but Señorita Molina told
us it could also mean "lifting" or "arising." They must
have been Pirates fans who came all the way from

Pittsburgh to see the game. Either that or they were taunting Clemente. He didn't seem to mind.

Everybody knows what to do on an 0-2 count. The batter has to protect the plate, swinging at just about anything close so he won't be called out on strikes. The pitcher will throw a ball out of the strike zone, hoping the batter will swing and miss at a bad pitch for strike three. I didn't bother explaining any of this to Sunrise. She wouldn't understand.

As predicted, the next pitch was outside, at least a few inches. I didn't think Clemente was going to swing at it; but at the last possible instant, he reached across the plate. It almost looked like his bat ripped the ball right out of the catcher's mitt.

When Clemente hit the ball, it made a different sound than when anybody else hit it. It sounded like a rifle shot. I didn't even see it leave the bat. But I did see the second baseman leap up with his glove fully extended. The ball went over his head, took a hop off the rightfield grass, and skipped all the way to the wall.

Stargell was sure to score from second, so I kept my eyes on Clemente. He didn't run like other people. As he broke from the batter's box, his legs were churning, his knees were pumping high, and his elbows were flailing out in every direction. But even so, he was fast and graceful. He ran like a wild colt.

As Clemente took the big turn around first, his batting helmet flew off his head. He didn't slow down. He hit the dirt feetfirst and slid past the second-base

His legs were churning, his knees were pumping high, and his elbows were flailing out in every direction.

bag, reaching up over his head to grab it with one hand. The throw coming in from the outfield wasn't even close.

"Wow!" Sunrise said after the umpire made the safe sign.

I think even she could appreciate the beauty of what we had just witnessed. The Cincinnati fans, of course, weren't nearly as appreciative, and they let loose a chorus of boos. Clemente jumped up and slapped the dirt off his pants. Stargell trotted across the plate for the first run of the game.

Pirates 1, Reds 0.

12

Royalty in Rightfield

AFTER CLEMENTE'S HIT, THE PIRATES WENT DOWN QUIETLY in the third inning. A vendor came around hawking popcorn, and Sunrise bought a bag. We munched on the popcorn while waiting for the Reds' turn at bat. I put my arm around her shoulder like guys do in the movies. She didn't push it away. All in all, things were going pretty well for a first date.

"How are you going to talk with Roberto Clemente?" Sunrise asked me. "You can't interrupt him in the middle of the game, can you?"

I had been asking myself the same question.

"Here's my plan," I told her. "I'm guessing the Pirates will be taking a bus back to their hotel after the game. We'll find the bus outside the ballpark and try to talk to him before he gets on it. If that doesn't work, we can try to go to the hotel."

"I'll help," Sunrise said.

The pitcher for the Pirates was Bob Moose. I recognized his name because one year I did a school project about baseball players who had animal names. There were a lot of them: Rabbit Maranville, Rob Deer, Catfish Hunter, Hippo Vaughn, Mule Haas, Steve Trout, Frank "Dodo" Bird. There was a guy named Turkey Tyson whose entire major-league career consisted of one at-bat for the Phillies in 1944. You could look it up.

And Bob Moose, of course.

Anyway, in the bottom half of the third, Moose didn't have his best stuff, and the Reds started a rally. It ended with Bobby Tolan smashing a three-run homer to give the Reds a 3-1 lead.

"I feel sorry for that guy," Sunrise told me as Tolan came around and stepped on home plate.

"You feel sorry for Bob Moose because he gave up a homer?" I asked.

"No," she said, "I feel sorry for the other guy. The guy who hit the ball."

"Tolan? He hit a three-run homer!" I said. "Why feel sorry for *him*?"

"Because he had to run all the way around the bases," she explained. "If you strike out, you get to go back to the dugout and sit down. It's not fair."

I couldn't help but laugh. She couldn't help but punch me in the arm.

Roberto Clemente came to bat again in the fifth inning. This time he hit an easy grounder to shortstop. Even though it was obvious to everyone in the ballpark that he was going to be thrown out, Clemente hustled down the line at full speed, as if somebody was chasing him with a knife. It was actually a close play at first.

That's what Flip always tells us: run hard, all the time. You never know when the shortstop might muff the play or the first baseman might drop the ball.

Clemente got two more singles in the game, but it wasn't his hitting that made him stand out from everyone else. It was the work he did in rightfield. He made a few plays that were just . . . impossible.

Like this one: In the fourth inning, the Reds had a runner at second base with one out. There was a left-handed batter at the plate, and he stroked a screaming liner to right. It was slicing as it streaked toward the rightfield corner.

A few feet away from the wall, he leaped.

Clemente was off with the crack of the bat, sprinting toward the foul line. A few feet away from the wall he leaped, his body fully extended and his back to home plate. The ball somehow stuck in the web of his glove, and he crashed into the wall at full speed.

But that was only half of it. The runner on second, seeing Clemente make the miraculous catch, tagged up and headed for third base. Clemente picked himself up off the dirt, spun around, and came up throwing. His arm was a blur. It was like a bullet flew out of it. All you could see was a white dot that came shooting out of the rightfield corner. The ball took a perfect one-hop and landed in the third baseman's glove. He didn't have to move it an inch. He swiped a tag on the runner as he slid into third.

When the umpire called the runner out, there was a gasp in the ballpark. Clemente had thrown the ball the length of a football field . . . for a strike. *Nobody* can throw a baseball that far, that accurately.

"*¡El magnifico!*" somebody shouted. Even the Reds fans were on their feet cheering after the play.

"Did you *see* that?" I asked Sunrise.

"Unbelievable," she agreed.

Then, picture this: In the fifth inning, a guy on the Reds hit a routine single to rightfield. Every outfielder knows what to do in that situation. You throw the ball to second base so the runner doesn't stretch a single into a double. Well, Clemente didn't play it that way.

He came charging in quickly to field the ball. But

instead of picking it up with his glove hand, he bare-handed it on the run. That way he didn't waste any time switching the ball over to his throwing hand. And instead of throwing to second base, he whipped the ball *behind the runner* to first. The runner had already made a turn at the first-base bag that was just a little too wide. By the time he realized the throw went to first, it was too late to get back. The first baseman tagged him out. Clemente had turned a hit into an out.

In the sixth inning, there was another single to right by the Reds. This time Clemente went to field the ball, but it ticked off his glove and bounced about ten feet away. The runner, seeing that the ball had been bobbled in rightfield, decided to try for second. But Clemente picked up the ball and gunned him down. I had no doubt that Clemente muffed the play *on purpose*, hoping the runner would take the bait and he would have the chance to throw the guy out at second. I had never heard of an outfielder deliberately making an error to fool a runner like that.

But the most amazing play of the game was in the bottom of the seventh inning. There were no outs. The Reds had runners at first and second. The Cincinnati pitcher was up. It was an obvious sacrifice situation. As expected, the pitcher squared around and bunted. It was a good one, past the pitcher's mound on the right side of the infield. Bob Moose couldn't field it. The Pirates second baseman was running to cover the base, so he couldn't get it. And the first baseman was covering the bag, so he couldn't get it either.

So who comes rushing in all the way from right-field to grab the ball? Clemente! He scooped it up and fired to third in time for the force play.

An *outfielder* involved in a bunt play? Un-heard of!

Clemente even had a flair when it came to flipping the ball in to the infield. He looped it in underhand. Nobody else did that.

I couldn't take my eyes off him the whole game. There was something different about the way Clemente swung the bat, ran the bases, chased after a fly ball, and threw, and even the way he walked out to right-field. It was recklessness combined with grace. And there was a quiet dignity to his manner.

"There's something almost royal about him," Sunrise said as Clemente jogged back to the Pirates dugout at the end of the seventh inning.

Royal. That was the word Flip had used when he'd been talking about Clemente. Flip said it was impos-sible to describe in words the way Clemente played the game. You had to see it with your own eyes. He was right. Now I had seen it.

I was glad that Sunrise got to witness such a great game for her first baseball experience. It was a seesaw battle the whole way. The Pirates scored once in the fourth inning to make it a one-run game, but the Reds picked up a run in the sixth and another one in the eighth. Then Pittsburgh tied it up in the ninth with three runs.

By that time, Clemente had been taken out of the game. I figured he might have injured himself making that circus catch in rightfield.

At the end of nine innings, it was tied at 5–5. Sunrise figured the game was over. I was explaining to her what "extra innings" meant when the Pirates went crazy in the tenth. A bunt, a couple of hits, an error, and a bases-loaded double by Carl Taylor, who had replaced Clemente, sealed the deal. The final score was Pittsburgh 12, Cincinnati 5.

Before Roberto Clemente left the game, he had three hits in four at-bats, one RBI, and a handful of amazing plays in rightfield. Not a bad day's work.

Sunrise and I got up to file out with the rest of the fans. She took my hand again. It had been a great game, and a great first date. I would always remember this night.

But I had something more important to think about. As we pushed through the exit turnstile at Crosley Field, I looked around for the Pirates' team bus. If I was ever going to talk to Roberto Clemente, this would be the time.

13

Fanatics

WHEN WE GOT OUTSIDE THE BALLPARK, WE HAD JUST ONE problem. There were at least 15 buses waiting for passengers, and there was no way to tell which one was waiting for the Pittsburgh Pirates.

Sunrise and I walked almost a complete circle around Crosley Field, hoping to find a bus driver we could talk to. A few of the buses pulled away. I had a growing sense of desperation. Maybe we had missed the Pirates. Maybe they weren't even going to a hotel. Maybe they would be heading straight to the airport to catch a flight to another city. Maybe I blew my chance to meet Roberto Clemente.

That's when I spotted a cluster of people gathered around an unmarked door near Gate D. Some of them were adults, but most were kids who looked younger than me. And all of them were holding pens and papers. Obviously, these were serious autograph collectors.

"C'mon!" I shouted, grabbing Sunrise's hand. "Follow me."

We hustled over to where the group was standing and tried to position ourselves close to the door. There were about 15 or 20 fans.

"Don't these people have anything better to do than hang around waiting for a guy to scrawl his name on a scrap of paper?" Sunrise whispered into my ear.

"That's why they're called fans," I told her. "It's short for 'fanatic.'"

A dumpy-looking lady and her dumpy-looking son were jostling for position in front of us. Both of them were wearing Cincinnati Reds hats.

"Remember to smile, Tommy," the mother said. "And always say 'please' and 'thank-you.'"

"Is this where the players come out?" Sunrise asked her.

"The visiting team usually comes out this exit," the lady replied. "The Reds use a different door, because most of them drive their cars home. But the security guards won't let us near there."

"The Pirates should be here in about five minutes," the boy added. "They have to shower and change their clothes first. I want to get Willie Stargell's autograph."

The two of them seemed to know what they were talking about. The boy was flipping through the pages of his autograph book. He probably had a signature from just about every player in the National League. It didn't seem to bother either of them that Sunrise and I were dressed like hippies.

"Do you know if Roberto Clemente talks with the fans?" Sunrise asked.

"Oh, yes, he's one of the nice ones," the lady said. "Some of these guys won't give you the time of day."

Everybody was waiting patiently; but after a few minutes, some people started getting antsy. There was a little pushing and shoving. A guy next to me wearing a camouflage jacket stepped on my toe. As I tried to get my foot out from under his, my hand brushed against his back.

"Hey, knock it off!" he said without even turning around to face me. "I was here first."

"Why don't you relax?" I told him.

"Yeah," Sunrise said, "we don't even want autographs."

The guy turned and looked at us. He was older than me, maybe 20. He had a crew cut.

"Then what are you doing here?" he asked.

"I want to talk to Roberto Clemente," I told him. "It's very important."

"It's a matter of life and death," added Sunrise.

"Then why don't you write him a letter?" the guy said. "The people who are here want autographs. We come to every game."

"It's a free country," Sunrise said. "We can go wherever we want. You don't own this spot, you know."

"Hey, be cool," I told Sunrise.

I could tell that this was the kind of guy you didn't want to get angry. Guys like him are just looking for somebody to fight.

"Why don't you go protest against something, buddy?" he said to me. "Dirty hippies."

I *did* look like a hippie, with my headband and love beads. And we were pretty dirty too, come to think of it. I couldn't remember the last time I had a shower. Sometime in the twenty-first century.

"Hey, why don't you leave him alone, mister?" Sunrise said. "He wasn't bothering you."

"Why doesn't he *make* me?" the guy with the crew cut said, pushing my shoulders back. "You wanna fight?"

The dumpy lady grabbed her son by the shoulder and pulled him away from us.

"No, I don't want to fight," I said.

"Of course you don't," the guy said. "You're a coward, like all those other freaks protesting against the war. But it's okay to let our soldiers fight and die so you can live in a free country, right?"

"The war is stupid," Sunrise told him. "*Nobody* should die. It's not even a real war. Only Congress has the power to declare war, and they never did. Do you know how many of our soldiers died in Vietnam last year? 16,000!"

"You know what's gonna happen if the Commies win?" the guy yelled. "The whole world will go Communist. It's because of unpatriotic traitors like you that our guys are dying and we're losing the war."

"It's because of morons like *you* that we have a war there in the first place!" Sunrise shot right back.

The guy cocked his fist.

"If you weren't a girl—" he said.

"Hey, leave her alone," I told him.

"Okay . . ."

That's when he hauled off and punched me in the nose.

I staggered backward. He had taken me completely by surprise. There were tears bubbling up in my eyes, but I didn't want to give him the satisfaction of seeing me wipe them away. I touched my nose. There was a trickle of blood on my fingers.

I've been in a few little skirmishes with kids my age, but I've never been flat-out punched in the nose by a grown man before. I'm usually pretty good about holding my temper. But when somebody socks you in the face, you can't just stand there and take it.

I charged at him and tried to punch his lights out, but he got his arm up quickly to protect his face. My best chance, I figured, was to go all out. I started flailing at him with both fists as fast and hard as I could. The more blows I threw, the more I would land. That was my strategy.

"Stop it!" Sunrise yelled, trying to pull us apart.

But I wasn't listening to her. Me and the crew cut guy were really going at it. I think I got a punch or two in there. But this guy was much stronger than me. And he knew how to fight. He managed to get me off my feet and onto the hard concrete.

He was on top of me now. He would be able to kick me or hit my head against the ground.

"Hey!" I heard the dumpy-looking lady say. "I'll bet the Pirates are coming out of Gate F tonight!"

Suddenly, everybody was rushing away. Even the guy who was on top of me got off and went running toward Gate F. Sunrise and I were all by ourselves. I was on the ground, and she was holding my head, trying to stop the bleeding.

"You don't have to do this," I told her, gasping for breath. "You should go home."

"It's all my fault," Sunrise said, sobbing. "I shouldn't have said a word to that jerk."

Sunrise cradled my head in her arms. It felt good to be taken care of. It was almost worth getting beaten up.

She was tending to my wounds when I looked over her shoulder to see a tall man standing behind her. I recognized him from pictures.

It was Roberto Clemente.

14

Dinner at El Cochinito

ROBERTO'S FACE LOOKED LIKE A SCULPTURE. HIS EYES WERE fierce and dark. His skin was smooth and shiny, like it had been stretched tightly over his bones. He could have been a movie star. I couldn't believe he was standing right in front of me.

His face looked like a sculpture.

Sunrise saw the look on my face and turned around.

"Is that . . . him?" she whispered. "Roberto?"

Ever since I'd left home, I had been mentally rehearsing what I would say if I was lucky enough to meet Roberto Clemente face-to-face. I didn't want to mess it up.

"*¡No subas el avion,* Roberto!" I said.

"What plane?" he replied, looking around. "Are you okay?"

"You speak . . . English?" I asked.

"Well, yeah. You need a doctor, man."

He spoke with an accent, but he wasn't hard to understand. His voice was soft.

"I heard you only spoke Spanish," I told him.

"People talk a lot of garbage," Roberto said. "Don't believe everything you hear."

He was dressed in white pants, a flowered silk shirt, and brown boots. He looked sharp. I noticed a thick book in his hand but couldn't make out the title.

"Tonight was my first baseball game," Sunrise told Roberto. "You were amazing."

"Thank you," he said. "What happened to your boyfriend here? Was he defending your honor?"

"He beat up a bully," Sunrise said. "He was very brave!"

Roberto called me her boyfriend, and Sunrise didn't dispute it! I was in heaven.

He put his book on the ground next to me and knelt on it so he wouldn't get his pants dirty. I looked at the title: *The Art of Chiropractic.* Huh! Interesting. My mom went to a chiropractor once for her sore back.

Roberto took a handkerchief out of his pocket.

"You should have ice on this," he said as he dabbed my nose with his handkerchief. "You know, fighting never solved any problems. But you can't let bullies push you around either. What are your names, anyway?"

"Joe Stoshack," I replied. "Stosh. And this is Sunrise."

Roberto shook hands with both of us and helped me get to my feet.

"It's pretty late for you kids to be wandering around," he said.

"We wanted to meet you," Sunrise said. "Where's the rest of your team?"

"Out," he said. "Drinking, chasing girls, looking for trouble. You know."

"Why aren't you with them?"

"Life is too short to waste time on nonsense," Roberto said.

I was surprised that he was wasting a minute on *me*. I figured I'd better get down to business while I had the chance.

"Mr. Clemente, there's something very important I need to talk to you about," I told him.

"Are you two hungry?" Roberto asked. "I know a Cuban place not too far from here. We can talk there."

"I don't have any money," I said.

"It's on me," he said. "C'mon."

Almost all of the fans had left the ballpark by that time. Roberto led us around a corner, where a taxicab was waiting.

Sunrise and I got in the backseat of the cab. Roberto got in the front and said something to the driver in Spanish.

Sunrise whispered in my ear, "We're going out to dinner with Roberto Clemente! Can you believe it?"

"So, Stosh," Roberto said as the cab pulled away. "You play ball?"

"Yeah," I told him, "but I'm in a batting slump. Right now I couldn't hit water if I fell out of a boat."

"Everybody slumps sometimes," Roberto said. "But I know a little trick that works for me."

"What is it?" I asked.

"Well, you've got to answer a question first," he said. "Who do you think has more chances to hit the ball: a batter who takes three swings—or a batter who takes one swing?"

"The guy who takes three swings, naturally," Sunrise said. "Even I know that."

"Of course," Roberto said. "So make sure you get three swings every time you come up to the plate. If you get four at-bats in a game, you'll get 12 swings. One good swing will break you out of that slump. You can't hit the ball if you don't swing at it. So don't let any strikes go by."

"But what if you don't get a good pitch to hit?" I asked.

"Just *swing*!" Roberto said. "They say I swing at bad balls. Well, if I hit 'em, I guess they weren't so bad, no?"

As he spoke, Roberto gestured with his hands. They were large, and he had long fingers—the kind you imagine a guitar player might have. When he lifted his left arm, I could see a big bruise on it.

"Did you get that when you crashed into the wall?" Sunrise asked. "It looks like it hurts."

"Everything hurts," Roberto said. "I got bone chips in my elbow, a curved spine, and arthritis. One of my legs is shorter than the other. I had malaria a few years ago. And I was in a bad traffic accident when I was in the minors. Every part of me hurts."

We pulled up outside a restaurant called El Cochinito. Roberto gave the cab driver a bill and told him to keep the change. We got out.

The manager of the restaurant greeted Roberto like an old friend and led us to a table in the corner. It was late, so there weren't many people in the place.

"You ever try fried bananas?" Roberto asked us.

"No, I just put bananas on my cereal," I replied.

"Well, you are in for a treat, my friend."

The menu was in Spanish, so Roberto ordered his favorite dishes for us: pork chops and crabs. He said he loved milk shakes, and gave specific instructions to the waiter to combine milk, a peach, egg yolks, banana ice cream, sugar, orange juice, and crushed ice in a blender.

Roberto seemed different from most of the other ballplayers I had met in my travels. Some of the guys—like Babe Ruth, Satchel Paige, Shoeless Joe Jackson, and Jackie Robinson—had big, exciting personalities. They seemed to fill any room they were in. But Roberto was quiet, serious, intense. He didn't smile a lot, crack jokes, or say outrageous things. There was an honesty and openness about him. He didn't seem as famous as he was.

I wondered why such an important man would be so nice to a couple of total strangers. Maybe he was lonely on the road. Maybe, because of his accent and culture, he couldn't relate very well to the other players on his team.

Or maybe he just needed somebody to boop his neck.

"I need you to boop my neck," he told us as we waited for our food to arrive.

"Huh?" I asked, figuring he said something in Spanish that I didn't understand.

"My disks," he said. "A vertebra in my neck and one in my lower back. They move. It's like a car with the wheels out of alignment. It doesn't drive right. After I hit the wall in rightfield, I knocked a couple of them out of position."

It made a certain amount of sense, I suppose.

Roberto took off his shirt and leaned forward over the table. He had a very muscular neck and wide shoulders.

Sunrise got up to rub Roberto's neck, but she wasn't doing it hard enough, and he asked me to take over. My mom knows a lot about massage. A few times when my muscles were really sore after a game, she would rub my back. The pain would melt away. She showed me how to do it.

It was hard to grab Roberto's skin because there was no extra fat on his body. I did the best I could, pushing and pulling at the flesh on his upper back.

"Dig your fingers in," Roberto told me. "Don't be afraid."

I worked harder, pushing my fingers against the bones of his neck until my own arms were sore. And then, suddenly, there was a *pop*. A boop. You could hear it. I took my hands away. I thought I might have broken something.

"What was *that*?" Sunrise asked.

"Ahhhhh," Roberto sighed. "*¡Excelente!*"

"Is it booped?" I asked.

"Yes, thank you," Roberto said as he put his shirt back on. "You did a good job, Stosh. Now, what can I do for you? What was that important thing you wanted to talk to me about?"

I looked at Sunrise, and she nodded to encourage me.

"You're going to find this hard to believe," I began, "but I don't live in this century. I live in the twenty-first century, in the future. I traveled through time to find you."

Roberto didn't laugh in my face, and I was grateful for that. He looked at me for a moment.

"And how did you do that, my friend?" he asked.

"With this," I said, pulling out my Roberto Clemente card. "I can travel back to the year on any card. This one is kind of messed up, but it got me here."

"You too?" Roberto asked Sunrise.

"No," she said. "I live here in Cincinnati. I ran away from home. I'm just helping Stosh."

"I believe in signs, omens," Roberto said. "In 1960 we were on a hot streak. Something said to me it was because of the sweatshirt I was wearing. So I didn't change that sweatshirt for two weeks. We won eleven games in a row."

The waiter came and put a bunch of food on the table. But none of us dug in yet.

"Why did you want to find me?" Roberto asked.

"I have bad news," I told him. "You're going to die."

"We're all going to die," Roberto said.

"Yes, but I know *when* you're going to die," I said. "It will be on New Year's Eve—"

"You must be confusing me with my brother Luis," Roberto said. "He died on New Year's Eve. It was 1954. He had a brain tumor."

I unzipped my backpack and took out the newspaper clipping Flip had given me.

"No," I said, handing him the article. "It will be three years from now, in a plane crash. You'll be on a mission to deliver food, medicine, and supplies to victims of an earthquake in Nicaragua."

Clemente Dies on Flight to Aid Managua

SAN JUAN, P.R., (UPI). — Baseball star Roberto Clemente and four other persons were killed late New Year's Eve when the DC-7 cargo plane the Pittsburgh Pirate idol had chartered for a mercy flight to quake-ravaged Nicaragua crashed into the Atlantic.

The four-engine, propeller-driven aircraft developed engine trouble after takeoff from San Juan. It was trying to return to the airport when it went down in 80 feet of water, about a mile off the coast.

A U.S. Coast Guard cutter and a Navy helicopter sent to the scene reported finding bits of wreckage, life jackets, luggage and boxes of relief supplies. The search for the victims' bodies was discontinued at nightfall and scheduled to be resumed at dawn.

CLEMENTE, 38, was a native and island hero of Puerto Rico, where three days of mourning were proclaimed.

He had been driven to the airport by his wife, Vera, 32.

She later said Clemente had been hesitant about making the flight to Managua, but told her: "What the heck, I'll go. Just be sure to have roast pork for me and the kids when I get back."

He is also survived by three children, Robert Jr., 7, Luisito, 5, and Ricky, 4.

The other victims were Arthur Rivera, president of

Continued on Page 4, Col. 3

Roberto read the first few paragraphs of the clipping, then looked up at me.

"Are you a seer?" he asked.

"In a way, I guess."

"He's trying to save your life," Sunrise said.

"I have seen more than enough death in my time," Roberto told us. "Besides Luis, my sister Anairis died from burns at five years old. Three years ago, two of my brothers died within a few weeks. I have always believed I would die before my time."

"I didn't want to tell you this," I said. "I'm sorry."

"So you're saying that if I try to save these people, I will die," Roberto said softly. "And if I let them die, then I will live?"

"Yes, basically."

"How many lives will be lost?" Roberto asked.

"Thousands," I said. "It's hard to say. Some will die immediately when the buildings collapse. Some will die afterward, from starvation or disease. Some probably would have died even if there hadn't been an earthquake."

Roberto pulled a card out of his pocket.

"This is what guides me," he said, handing me the card. There was handwriting on it:

If you have a chance to accomplish something that will make things better for people coming behind you, and you don't do that, you are wasting your time on this earth.

"I like to work with kids," Roberto continued. "I'd like to work with kids all the time if I live long enough. When I was your age, we couldn't afford to buy a baseball. So we hit empty soup cans. My first glove was a coffee-bean sack. Someday, I want to build a sports city for the poor kids of Puerto Rico. There will be ballfields, a swimming pool, and a lake. The kids will get involved with sports instead of drinking and drugs. They'll learn about being good citizens and respecting their parents. That is my dream."

Roberto filled our plates with food and then his own.

"What about donating money?" Sunrise suggested. "Instead of flying to Nicaragua, you could give money to the Red Cross or some other organization, and they could deliver the food and medicine to the earthquake victims."

"Money is pieces of paper," Roberto said. "It is paying someone to do the dirty work so you don't have to."

He stopped talking and dug into his food. I tried the pork chops and crabs. They were really good. I didn't want to try the fried banana, but Sunrise said it was tasty and insisted that I have a bite. It was okay, but a little strange. Too sweet for me. The milk shake was great, though.

I thought about what Roberto had said. It was hard to argue with him. He was determined to use his celebrity to help people and make the world a better place. But I was determined too. And I knew that if he got on that plane, he would die.

"You won't be able to help *anybody* if you're not alive," I told him. "You won't be able to start a sports city for kids. You can do so much more good for people if you don't go to Nicaragua."

Roberto stopped eating and looked at me.

"You are stubborn," he said. "Like me. You went through a lot to deliver this message to me. I respect that." Roberto paused before adding, "Okay, Stosh. I will do as you say."

I let go a breath of air that I must have been holding in for an hour. Sunrise smiled and nodded to me. We finished eating quietly. I didn't want to say anything that might screw up what I had accomplished.

The waiter brought the check. Roberto paid it and

asked if the owner of the restaurant could call him a taxicab. He told us he was tired and had to go back to the hotel. The Pirates were scheduled to fly to Houston in the morning to play the Astros.

"I want to give you something," he said as we walked outside.

"You've already given us so much," Sunrise said.

Roberto pulled a hundred-dollar bill out of his wallet and stuffed it in my hand.

"For your doctor bills when you get home," he said.

"I couldn't possibly—" I started to say, but he pushed my fingers closed around the bill.

"It was because of me that you got hurt," he said.

"You don't have to do that," I told him.

"I know."

Roberto hugged us both. A cab pulled up and he got in. He said something in Spanish to the driver. Before the cab pulled away, Roberto rolled down the window.

"And you," he said to Sunrise, "go back to your home and family. Family is more important than any game. It is all we have. Family is everything."

Roberto waved to us as the cab pulled away.

15

Good-bye

I DIDN'T FEEL SAD WHEN ROBERTO LEFT. JUST THE OPPOSITE. Such a feeling of satisfaction came over me. I had done what I had set out to do. Once we found our way to Cincinnati, it had all been fairly easy, really. I was lucky enough to meet Roberto Clemente. He didn't think I was a crackpot. He saw that what I was saying made sense. And he agreed not to get on the plane. So I had accomplished my mission. Now it was time to go home.

There was just one problem: Sunrise.

We were sitting on a bench in front of El Cochinito. It was dark out and probably close to midnight. The streets were almost empty. It was quiet. The lights went out inside the restaurant. It had been some night. Sunrise and I would be going our separate ways. We both knew it. She put her arms around me.

I know I'm too young to fall in love with anybody. But I liked Sunrise a lot. We had fun together. I felt completely at ease with her. I didn't have to wonder if I was saying the right thing all the time or what she was trying to tell me.

I don't have a lot of friends at home in Louisville. If I met somebody like Sunrise back home, she would definitely be my best friend. I didn't want to leave her, especially after all we had been through together.

"That would be so amazing if you actually changed history tonight," she said.

"I hope I did," I replied. "I guess I'll find out when I get home."

"It must be exciting, being able to do what you do," she said quietly. "Does anybody else in the future have the power to travel through time with baseball cards?"

"Not that I know of."

"I guess you can take stuff with you, huh?" she asked. "Your backpack, your clothes, and all. It would be pretty funny if you went back in time and your clothes didn't go with you."

"It would be," I said, imagining it. "I don't know if there's a weight limit. Like on an airplane when they weigh your suitcase."

"Is it possible to take a person with you?" Sunrise asked.

"Yeah," I told her. "I took my mom with me one time. My dad too. Oh, and my baseball coach, Flip Valentini."

I finally realized that Sunrise was dropping hints. She wanted to go home with me. Maybe she liked me as much as I liked her. Or maybe she just wanted to see the future. I couldn't blame her. I always wanted to travel to the future too. But that's impossible, of course. I would need to have a future baseball card, and they haven't been printed yet.

"I wish I could see one of those VD players you were telling me about," she said.

"That's DVD," I corrected her.

"Yeah, one of those. They sound cool."

There were so many reasons why it would be a big mistake to take Sunrise to the twenty-first century with me. She would never see her friends or family again. That would be the biggest reason. They would report her as missing, if they hadn't already. It would be all over the news. People would think she had been kidnapped. The police would waste a lot of time and money searching for her. As time went by, her parents would assume she was dead. That would be a terrible thing to do to them.

I also had to consider how jumping to the twenty-first century would change Sunrise's life. She wouldn't finish her education. She would miss four decades of history that she should have lived through. And what if she was going to have children of her own someday? They would never be born. Or they would be born 50 years later. It would be very risky to take her along.

On the other hand, she was *really* pretty.

"Do you . . . want to come with me?" I finally asked.

"You would take me?" she said, looking up with those great eyes of hers.

I opened my backpack and took out my new baseball cards. I tore off the wrapper and picked a card out of the stack.

"Hold my hand," I said, "and close your eyes."

I explained to Sunrise that nothing would happen for a minute or two. And then, gradually, she would begin to feel a tingling sensation in her fingertips. That was the signal that we would be going to the year on the card.

"And then what happens?" she asked. "We . . . *vanish*? Just like that?"

"Yeah, just like that."

"Okay," she said, taking a deep breath, "let's go."

I felt a tingling sensation right away. But that was only because I still wasn't used to holding hands with a pretty girl. Soon that feeling was replaced by the other tingling sensation, the one I was used to. It tickled my fingernails.

"Do you feel anything yet?" Sunrise whispered.

"Yeah," I said. "Just relax. Think of the future. The twenty-first century. Think of Louisville, Kentucky."

That's what I was doing. The vibrations were getting more powerful, moving up my arm, across my chest, and down my other arm to the hand Sunrise was holding.

"I feel something!" she said suddenly.

"Shhhhh!"

My whole body was starting to vibrate. We were approaching the point of no return. And then . . .

I pulled my hand away and let go of the card.

"What?" she asked. "Did something go wrong?"

"I can't do it," I told her.

"Why not?"

"Roberto was right," I said. "You should be home with your family. It would be wrong to just rip somebody out of their world like this."

Sunrise sighed. It looked like her eyes were moist.

"I don't want to go home to my parents," she said softly. "And school starts in a few weeks. I want to get out of here. I want to go with you."

"Do you love your parents?" I asked.

Sunrise took a moment to think it over. Then she nodded her head.

"My mom and I fight all the time," I told her. "It's even worse with my dad. Everybody has problems getting along with their parents. It's, like, part of growing up."

"I know, I know," she said.

"Look, in a few years, you'll be finished with high school and off to college," I told her. "You've got your whole life ahead of you. And you know what? You're gonna see DVDs and all that other stuff for yourself. You're 14 now. So you'll be 24 in 1979, 34 in 1989, 44 in 1999, and 54 in 2009. You can get a DVD player then. And a flat-screen TV that just about fills a whole wall. Hey, maybe you can invite me over and we'll watch movies together."

"But I'll be old," she said, "and you'll be a teen-ager."

"We can still be friends."

"Okay," she said with a sigh. "But will you do one favor for me?"

"What?" I asked.

"Let me watch?"

I don't usually let people watch me travel through time. It would be weird to see somebody disappear before your eyes. But this was special. I told her it would be okay.

"I'll miss you," she said.

"I'll miss you too."

After Sunrise assured me she would be able to take a cab home, I picked up the baseball card again. I closed my eyes and concentrated on going home. It didn't take long for the tingling sensation to come back. It was like it had just been interrupted.

"Is it happening?" Sunrise whispered. I felt her breath on my ear.

"Yeah," I said, "it's happening."

The vibrations washed over me as if I was lying at the edge of the beach and a wave came in.

"Good-bye, Stosh," I heard Sunrise say.

And just before I disappeared, I felt her lips press against mine.

Then I was gone.

16

Homecoming

I CAME FLYING INTO THE LIVING ROOM. MY FOOT HIT THE floor at a strange angle. I reached out to grab something to steady myself, but there was nothing there. I tripped over the coffee table and did an X Games–quality face plant at the foot of the stairs just as Mom was coming down from the second floor with a basket of laundry. She stared at me for a second with a funny look on her face, like I was wearing a clown nose or something.

"Is it Halloween already?" she asked.

I looked at myself. The love beads were still around my neck. I pulled off the headband.

"Mom! You won't believe it! I was at Woodstock!" I exclaimed. "It was *so* cool! And I went to Cincinnati in a Volkswagen van with some hippies. And I saw Jimi Hendrix play!"

"No way!" she gushed.

"Yes way!" I insisted. "He played 'The Star-Spangled Banner' and 'Purple Haze'!"

"I *knew* I should have gone with you!" my mother said. "You didn't tell me you were going to Woodstock. You just said you were going to save Roberto Clemente."

"I was. I mean, I did!" I said. "Or I think I did, anyway. I got kind of blown off course somehow. Did you see anything on the news about Clemente?"

"No," she said. "Like what?"

Well, of course she hadn't seen anything on the news about Clemente. The news only reports on planes that crash, not on ones that land safely. They report when people die tragically, not when they live peacefully.

"I'll be right back," I said, rushing past her upstairs, taking two steps at a time.

It would be a simple matter to go on the Internet and find out whether or not I had changed history.

I was feeling optimistic when I turned on my computer. For once, I had accomplished my mission. Roberto was only 38 years old when he died. If he didn't get on that plane in 1972, he probably would have played a few more seasons and padded his statistics, which were already so impressive.

He may even still be alive, it occurred to me. I did the arithmetic in my head. Roberto was born in 1934. So if he lived into the millennium, he would have been 66 at that time. It was entirely possible that he was still living, now an old man. And it would be because of me.

The more hurried I am, the slower my computer runs. What's up with that? Finally I got online and googled ROBERTO CLEMENTE. There were over four million websites that mentioned his name. I clicked on the first one, and there it was:

```
Born: August 18, 1934
Died: December 31, 1972
```

No! It couldn't be! He shouldn't have died in 1972! I saved him! He said he wouldn't get on the plane!

I clicked down to the second website.

```
Died: December 31, 1972
```

And the third.

```
Died: December 31, 1972
```

It was the same for every one I tried. Nothing was different. I didn't change history. Despite everything I went through, Roberto *still* died in that plane crash. I cursed as I smashed my fist against the desk.

I couldn't help but be angry. I was angry with Roberto. He deceived me. He ignored my warning that the plane was going to crash. He went ahead and got on it, anyway.

My mother came rushing upstairs.

"Are you okay?" she asked. "I heard a bang."

"Roberto lied to me!" I told her. "He said he wouldn't

go to Nicaragua! But he got on the plane anyway; and now he's dead. He should have listened to me!"

"Joey . . ."

"And what good did it do?" I continued. "He didn't help the victims of that earthquake. All the medicine and stuff he was going to deliver to them must have ended up in the ocean. Roberto sacrificed his life for nothing."

My mother leaned over from behind and wrapped her arms around me.

"It wasn't for nothing," she said. "I bet he inspired a lot of people to do good things. Just like he inspired you. That's the only positive thing about tragedy, Joey. It makes the survivors better people. This just shows how good a man he must have been; he would go help strangers even though he knew he would most likely die doing it."

"You think so?" I asked.

"Either that," she said, laughing, "or maybe he just figured you were nuts. That's what I would think if some kid with love beads told me he comes from the future and knows when I'm going to die."

"Yeah," I said. "He probably figured I was just a crazy hippie kid."

"A *tired* crazy hippie kid," my mother said, kissing the top of my head. "You can save the world another day, Joey. Go to sleep. Flip called, by the way. You've got a game tomorrow night, you know. And be sure to put your dirty clothes in the hamper. I'm in the middle of doing the laundry."

Mom closed the door, and I put my computer to sleep. I was still a little upset. What was the use? I tried to do something good for the world, and this was the result.

Maybe it never happened, it suddenly occurred to me. Maybe I never even went back to 1969. What if it was all a dream? What if I really *am* crazy?

It had been a long day, a long couple of days. I needed a shower.

I pulled off my jeans and put them in the hamper. Then I remembered that I needed to go through the pockets carefully. One time I left a pen in my pocket; and when my mom washed the clothes, there was blue ink all over the dryer. She was pretty mad.

The first three pockets of my jeans were empty, but the back right pocket had some pieces of paper in it. I pulled them out. One of the papers had this on it:

If you have a chance to accomplish something that will make things better for people coming behind you, and you don't do that, you are wasting your time on this earth.

The other paper looked like this:

So it wasn't a dream. It really happened.

17

An Unexpected Visitor

IT WAS HARD TO SLEEP THAT NIGHT. I KEPT THINKING ABOUT everything that had happened over the last couple of days—my talk with Señorita Molina, Woodstock, Jimi Hendrix, Sunrise, Peter and Wendy, the game at Crosley Field, and of course meeting Roberto Clemente.

There's a little night-light plugged in near the door of my room. It's not that I'm afraid of the dark. What I'm afraid of is smashing my toe against the furniture in the dark. I did that once and nearly had to go to the emergency room. The night-light gives off just enough light to see my way around.

At some point in the middle of the night, I woke up. There was a noise, I think. I looked at the clock next to my bed. It said it was 2:14. Then I looked across the room, over at my desk.

There was somebody sitting there.

In the dark.

Looking at me.

I didn't freak out. It had to be a dream. How else could somebody get into my room in the middle of the night?

The night-light was bright enough for me to tell that the person at my desk wasn't my mom. And it wasn't my Uncle Wilbur, who lives with us. It looked like a boy, about my age. He was just sitting there.

"Are you awake?" the boy whispered, leaning forward in my chair.

"I'm not sure," I replied honestly. "If this is a dream, then no."

"Are you Joseph Stoshack?" the boy asked.

"Yeah," I replied. "Who are you?"

"My name is Bernard," he said. "Bernard Stoshack."

"Are you related to me?" I asked.

"Yeah," he replied. "I'm your great-grandson."

Well, now I *knew* I was dreaming. I'm 13 years old. I'm not married. I don't have kids, much less grandkids. Either I was having a dream, or somebody was playing a very elaborate practical joke on me.

"That's funny," I said.

"I know this probably sounds a little crazy," said the boy, "but I'm telling you the truth. You're my great-grandfather. I live in the year 2080."

Oh, this kid was *good*. I looked around the room for the blinking red light of a video camera. There had to be one somewhere. This would probably be on

YouTube by morning. I figured I might as well play along.

"Um-hmm," I said. "And how did you get here, Bernard Stoshack . . . or whatever your name is?"

"I climbed in the window," he replied.

"No," I said. "I mean, if you come from the year 2080, how did you get *here*, to my time? Did you walk? Did you fly?"

"No," he replied. "I used a baseball card."

"What!?"

"I know you have the power to travel through time with a baseball card," he explained. "So do I. My father couldn't do it. Neither could my grandfather. But it must be genetic, because I have the same power that you do. It must have skipped a couple of generations."

"What gave you the idea that I can travel through time with a baseball card?" I asked.

"I read it in your diary," he replied.

Ha! Now I *knew* the kid was a phony.

"I don't even keep a diary!" I said.

"You will," he told me, "when you're an old man. You'll want to tell your children, and your grandchildren, that you have this gift. You'll want to alert them that they might have the same power as you. And I do, Grandpa! Whenever I pick up an old baseball card and hold it in my hand, something strange happens. I get this tingling sensation in the tips of my fingers. Then it moves across my body. It feels almost like . . . like waves on the beach."

I fell back against my pillow.

"I know the drill," I said. "Let me see the card you used."

My eyes had adjusted to the light somewhat. He pulled a card out of his pocket and showed it to me. It was an Alex Rodriguez card, a little beat up and yellowed; but it looked real.

"You say you found this in the year 2080 and used it to get here?" I asked.

"That's right," he said. "I found it a few weeks ago in an old trunk filled with your diary and some other stuff. But I had a heck of a time finding you, Grandpa. I live in Chicago. I thought the card was going to take me right here. But I landed downtown at the Louisville Slugger Museum and had to figure out where you lived. As I was walking over here, some guys tried to rob me and I ran away. I almost got killed. Did anything like that ever happen to you, Grandpa?"

It *had* to be a dream. That was the only possible explanation. The only person I know who can describe the time travel process so accurately is *me*. Even my mother doesn't know exactly how it works.

I looked at the clock again. It was 2:16.

Usually I don't remember my dreams. They seem so real while they're happening. Then I wake up in the morning with this vague memory that I had a dream but with no idea what it was about. This one was particularly vivid.

I should write it down, I thought, *so I won't forget*

it. But it's too much trouble to get out of bed to find a piece of paper and a pen when you're so tired. I promised myself I would remember. It would be fun to tell my mother about this one in the morning.

Bernard went on and on, talking about everything he went through to find my house in the middle of the night, how he climbed the tree outside my window and crept into my room.

What a great dream, I thought, as he kept right on talking. If only it was real. It would be cool to actually meet my great-grandchildren.

I rolled over and fell back asleep.

I don't know how much time passed, but I was lying there in bed for a while and something caused me to wake up again. I punched the pillow and tried to get comfortable. All I wanted to do was get some sleep. If I didn't fall asleep soon, I knew I would feel lousy all day. And I had a game to play that night.

I looked at the clock—2:19. This was going to be a long night.

"Grandpa . . ." a voice whispered.

Startled, I looked across the room. The kid was still there!

I bolted up from my bed.

"Get out of—"

The kid leaped to his feet and clapped one hand over my mouth before I could get out another word. He pushed his other hand against the back of my head and held it tight, like a clamp. He was strong, stronger than me. He didn't smell very good. This wasn't any dream. Now I was freaking out.

"Is everything okay, Joey?" my mom called from down the hall.

"Tell her everything's okay," the boy whispered.

He took his hand off my mouth.

"Everything's okay, Mom," I said. "I was just having a dream."

"Now, *shhhhhh!*" the boy whispered, putting his hand back over my mouth. "You're *not* dreaming! I know you're scared right now. I'm sorry I had to do it this way, but I didn't know what else to do. You've got to listen to me. I know it's hard to believe. My name is Bernard Stoshack, and I'm 13 years old, okay? You are my great-grandfather. I live in the year 2080, and I have the same power as you to travel through time with baseball cards. This is not a hoax. It's for real. You got it?"

I nodded my head, and he let go. I flipped on the light next to my bed to get a better look at him. He was dressed in ratty old clothes—torn, faded jeans and a striped shirt that should have been turned into a rag a long time ago. I searched his face for a family resemblance. He looked a little like me, I suppose. Dark hair. Kind of big ears. Stocky. It was hard to tell. He could have been anybody.

"Prove you're who you say you are," I demanded.

He pulled out a wallet from his pocket and produced a library card. CHICAGO PUBLIC LIBRARY, it said at the top. His picture was below it, next to the name

BERNARD STOSHACK. I looked to see when the card was due to expire—February 2082.

Maybe the kid *was* for real. But I wasn't completely convinced. It could still be a hoax. It would be easy to make a fake library card. The question was, why would anyone bother?

"I know everything about you, Grandpa," he told me. "Your parents' names are Terry and Bill. They got divorced when you were nine years old. Your mom is a nurse. She works at Louisville Hospital. Your dad was in a traffic accident that paralyzed him. Your favorite thing in the world is playing baseball. Your coach's name is Flip Valentini. I could go on if you want me to."

I was beginning to believe that he was the real deal. Still, it was hard for me to wrap my mind around the idea that my own great-grandson was sitting right next to me . . . and that he was the same age as me! I went to give him a hug, and he hugged me back.

"Why are you here?" I asked.

"Shhhhh!" Bernard said. "You'll wake Grandma . . . I mean, your mother."

"Did you come here just to meet me?" I whispered.

"No," he replied.

Why would somebody from the year 2080 travel back to our time? I wondered. There could be lots of reasons. It would be pretty cool, for one thing. But time travel is too risky to do just for kicks. Bernard must be on a mission, I decided—just like I always give myself a mission to accomplish when I travel through time.

"Then why are you here?" I repeated.

"I can't tell you right now."

"Why not?" I asked.

"Shhhhhh!" Bernard said urgently. "I need to show you something. I need you to come with me."

"Where?" I asked.

"To 2080," he said. "I need to take you to the future, Grandpa."

18

The Future Is Ours to See

THE FUTURE!

Ever since my first experience traveling through time, I dreamed of going to the future. If I could move backward in time, why not forward? Common sense says I should be able to go in either direction. But, of course, I knew why that was impossible.

"How can I travel to the future?" I asked Bernard. "I would need a future baseball card."

"I know," he replied. "I have one."

He reached into his back pocket and pulled out a piece of gray cardboard that was a little bigger than a baseball card. Actually, it was two pieces of cardboard taped together on three sides. He tapped it a few times until the edge of a card popped out the side that wasn't taped. The card fell on my bed, faceup. I wondered why Bernard didn't just keep his baseball cards in plastic sleeves the way I do.

I went to pick up the card, but Bernard pushed my hand away.

"Don't touch it, Grandpa!" he warned me. "Not yet. You know what happens when we touch it."

I pointed my light at the card and leaned over to examine it.

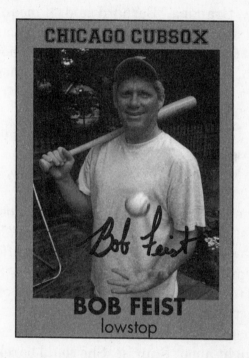

"Bob Feist?" I said. "I never heard of this guy."

"Of course not," Bernard said. "He hasn't been born yet. Bob Feist plays in *my* time. He's one of my favorite players. This card is what I brought along to take me back home, and to take you into the future, Grandpa."

"Do you have to call me Grandpa?" I asked.

"But that's who you are," Bernard said. "You're my great-grandfather."

"It's creepy," I told him. "I'm 13."

"Well, what do you want me to call you?"

"Stosh," I said. "Just call me Stosh."

"Okay, Grandpa," Bernard said. "I mean, Stosh."

"Wait a minute," I said, looking at the card again. "Chicago *Cubsox*? You don't mean to tell me—"

"Yeah, the Cubs and the White Sox merged into one team a long time ago," said Bernard. "It was around 2050. It's a long story."

"Wow," I said, "people in Chicago must have been really upset."

"They're used to dealing with adversity," Bernard said.

I leaned over to study the card more closely.

"Lowstop?" I asked. "What's a lowstop?"

"The word 'shortstop' was considered offensive by midgets and dwarves," Bernard told me. "So it was changed to 'lowstop.' There have been a lot of changes in the last 70 years."

"I'll bet."

I thought about Sunrise. She could barely picture all the things we have in the twenty-first century: DVDs, IMAX, iPods, the Internet. In 1969, the PC hadn't even been invented yet. And that was only a few decades ago. I couldn't imagine how much the world would change and technology would advance

70 years from now. In Bernard's world, it was probably like *Star Wars* every day.

Bernard got up and started looking curiously at the stuff on my desk, picking things up and putting them down. It occurred to me that my room must look like an antique shop to him. Or maybe one of those living-history museums.

"Do you have a flying car?" I asked him.

"Hmmm?" Bernard had picked up a calculator from my desk and was engrossed in punching the buttons.

"A flying car," I repeated. "They say that in the future, every family will have a car that flies. Do you have one of those?"

"Uh, no," he replied.

"Too bad," I said. "It would be cool to ride in one. But I bet you have lots of other great stuff, huh? Like robot servants and microwave freezers. How about light sabers and laser guns? Do you have them?"

"You'll find out when we get there," Bernard said absentmindedly. He was looking at my cell phone charger.

"What about a jet pack?" I asked. "I bet you have your own jet pack, right?"

"A what?" Bernard asked.

"A jet pack," I said. "You know, one of those things you strap to your back so you can go flying around? Do you jet pack to school every day?"

"No," he said, "I don't have a jet pack."

"Oh," I said. "Too bad. Hey, can we go now? I can't wait to see what the future will be like."

I pulled on a pair of jeans and took a clean T-shirt from my drawer.

"Give me just one minute, Grandpa," Bernard said.

"Don't call me Grandpa!" I said.

"Shhhhhhhhhhh!"

Bernard seemed fascinated by the ordinary stuff in my room. He found the switch on my desk lamp and turned it on. Then he turned it off again. Then he turned it back on and looked at the bulb.

"You probably don't even need light switches in the future, huh?" I asked. "You probably turn your lights on and off through mind control or something, right? You just think 'On' and the light goes on. Man, future stuff is cool."

"Um-hmm," he mumbled.

Bernard didn't seem interested in talking about what the world is like in 2080. He looked at my electric pencil sharpener, my laptop, my iPod.

"This stuff must look like a lot of old junk to you, huh?" I asked. "I bet you have much cooler stuff in 2080. Futuristic stuff."

"Okay," Bernard said with a sigh, "I've seen enough. We need to go."

I was curious why he always used the word "need." It was never "We *should* go" or "I would *like* to take you to the future." It was always "We *need* to go" and "I *need* to take you to the future."

We both knew what to do. Bernard turned off the desk lamp and sat on my bed next to me. I grabbed his hand and closed my eyes.

"Aren't you forgetting something?" he asked.

"What?"

"Some baseball cards?" he said.

"Oh, yeah. Of course."

I went to my desk and got a pack of new baseball cards out of the drawer. My ticket back home. I put them in my pocket and sat down on the bed again.

"Do you want to hold the Bob Feist card?" he asked me. "We both have the power. I suppose it doesn't really matter which one of us holds the card."

Usually I'm the one who is taking somebody with me through time. I had never been a "passenger" before.

"You hold it," I said. "I want to see what it's like to go along for the ride."

Bernard took my hand with his right hand and picked up the card with his left. My hand was sweaty, and I realized I was nervous. I took a deep breath and closed my eyes.

"This will take a few minutes," Bernard said.

"I know," I said. "Hey, I just remembered. I have a game tomorrow night."

"I'll get you back in time," Bernard told me.

While I waited for the tingling sensation to come, I concentrated on the future. If Bernard read a diary that I kept as an old man, he must know a lot about me. He knew things that I didn't even know about myself. There was so much I wanted to ask him. What did I grow up to do for a living? Was I successful at it? I must have gotten married. Who was my wife? How many children did we have? And, of course, when did I die?

Bernard probably had a lot of questions he wanted to ask me too. But there would be time for that once we got to 2080.

"It's starting to happen," Bernard suddenly said.

"You feel the tingling sensation?" I asked.

"Yeah," he replied, "in my fingertips."

"It won't be long now," I said.

"It's moving up my arm," he whispered.

I knew exactly what he was experiencing. After a minute or so, my left hand—the one he was holding—started to tingle. The sensation quickly moved across my body and down my legs. We were approaching the point of no return.

"In the future," I whispered, "is everything, like, in 3-D and stuff?"

"You'll see very soon, Grandpa," Bernard replied.

"Don't call me Grandpa!"

And then we disappeared.

19

So Much for Science Fiction

BERNARD AND I LANDED IN A FIELD. IT WAS A BASEBALL field, but it took me a moment or two to figure that out. It wasn't a nicely mowed and groomed field like the ones I play on. There was no backstop, no fences, and no bleachers. It was more like a vacant lot.

There was a piece of cardboard where first base would be. Somebody's shirt was second base. An old shoe was third. And home plate was a garbage can cover.

"Are you okay?" Bernard asked, brushing the dirt off his pants.

"Yeah, I think so," I said.

A bunch of boys were throwing high pops to one another in the outfield. They seemed to be about my age. I looked around. There was a house in the distance, a barn, a silo, and some trees—but not much else. We were out in the country somewhere.

What was going on? I looked up to the sky to see if there were any cars or people flying around with jet packs. There was nothing up there. Not even planes. Something must have gone wrong. Well, that figured. Something *always* goes wrong. Why is it that I never land where I want to land?

"Didn't you say you live in Chicago?" I asked Bernard.

"I do," he replied. "This *is* Chicago."

"Where's the Sears Tower?" I asked. I remembered reading that the Sears Tower was one of the tallest buildings in the world, and that it was in Chicago.

"It's gone," Bernard said. "It was gone before I was born."

I wanted to press him for details, but the boys in the outfield came running over. They all had on ratty old clothes like Bernard. Some of them were barefoot. I was glad I had just thrown on a pair of jeans. If I had gotten dressed up, I would have looked like I was going to a wedding compared to these guys.

"Hey, Bernard!" one of the boys shouted. "Where were you? Let's play ball. Who's the kid?"

"This is my gr—" Bernard began, but I interrupted him.

"Cousin," I said. "Joe Stoshack. I'm from Louisville. Call me Stosh."

I didn't know if people still shook hands with each other in 2080. Bernard had told me that a lot had changed in 70 years. For all I knew, they pulled each other's ears or had some other bizarre greeting. But they all came over to say hello and shake my hand, just like back home. They seemed like good guys.

We divided into two teams, and I was put on Bernard's team. There were only enough for seven players per team, so everybody agreed to having one roving outfielder. We were up first. The other team ran out to the field.

As I watched the pitcher warm up, I realized how hot it was outside. It must have been close to a hundred degrees. Ordinarily, I try not to go out when it's that hot. I'd rather stay inside with the air-conditioning on. But nobody else seemed to mind. It must be the middle of a summer heat wave, I figured. The sun was high in the sky.

"The new kid gets to bat first," one of the guys said.

"Go get 'em, Gramps," Bernard whispered in my ear.

There was no bat rack, just a garbage can with six bats in it. All of the bats were made of wood. I picked up one of the smaller ones. It felt heavy.

"No metal bats anymore?" I asked Bernard.

"Nah, we're baseball purists," he replied. "This is the way the game was meant to be played."

I took some practice swings, choking up a few inches on the bat. With a heavier bat, I knew I would have to get it moving a little quicker to make contact.

"Come on, Stosh, hammer it!" somebody on my team hollered.

"Hit one into the next century!" Bernard yelled.

For all I knew, in 70 years, pitchers might have developed some new trick pitches that would totally fool me. I decided to let the first two go by before taking a swing. That's what I did, and the catcher called both of them strikes. The second pitch looked a little outside to me, but I didn't argue about it. I didn't want to look like a jerk.

I also didn't want them to think I couldn't hit. So I was determined to take a rip at the next pitch if it was anywhere close to the plate.

"Three strikes and you're out, Stosh!" somebody yelled. "Protect the plate."

Well, at least the rules of baseball were the same. It would have been embarrassing if they had changed it to four strikes or something like that.

The pitcher went into the standard windup and threw the next one right down the pipe. I hacked at it and slapped a hard grounder to the left side of the infield.

I didn't look to see if the shortstop or third baseman fielded the ball. I just put my head down and dug for first. Safe by a mile! There was no throw.

But when I crossed the first-base bag and turned around, everyone was in hysterics. I mean, they were falling all over one another with laughter. It was like the funniest thing they had ever seen. Tears were running down their faces.

"What?" I asked. "What did I do?"

"Is that how they play ball in Louisville?" one guy said, doubled over.

Bernard came jogging over to me. He put his arm around my shoulder.

"Uh, Grandpa," he whispered. "There's one thing I forgot to mention. They changed the rules slightly. You don't run to first base anymore. You're supposed to run to *third*. Then second. Then first. And home. Like that."

"What?" I asked in disbelief. "You run around the bases *backward*? That's dumb! Why did they change the rules?"

"For the novelty of it, I guess," Bernard said. "I don't know, to tell you the truth. It happened about 40 years ago."

Everybody was still doubled over laughing, and my face was probably as red as a fire engine. But the guys were fair about it. They let me go back and have a do over because I didn't know the rules.

The count was still 0-2. I dug in at the plate—or the garbage can cover, anyway—and gripped the bat tightly. I was determined not to make a fool of myself again. The pitcher asked if I was ready; and when I nodded my head, the ball suddenly came flying out from behind his back. He didn't even wind up. The next thing I knew, the ball had plopped into the catcher's mitt. I never got the bat off my shoulder.

"Strike three!" yelled the catcher. "You're out!"

I trudged back and sat down next to Bernard.

"Is that pitch legal?" I asked.

"We play by jungle rules," he told me. "Anything goes."

Jungle rules? I never heard of anything like that.

It was okay, though. The game was still fun. Baseball is baseball. I just had to get used to a few changes. For instance, one kid on each team was the "designated fielder." That meant he would play the field but not come to bat.

When the other team was up, I borrowed a glove and they put me at shortstop—I mean, lowstop. When the first grounder came my way, I threw the ball to first base out of instinct. Everybody fell all over themselves laughing again. But after an inning or two, I got used to the new rules. I didn't get any hits, but I made a couple of nice plays at "low," and we were winning by three runs when some of the guys said they had to go home. So we ended the game there.

Everybody said good-bye and walked or rode their bikes down the dirt road leading away from the field. Nobody's parents came to pick them up, I noticed. Bernard gave me a rag to wipe the sweat off my face.

"Come on," he said when everybody was gone. "I'll show you around."

At last! Finally, I would get to see Bernard's cool future stuff. I figured that his cell phone was probably the size of a fingernail and his iPod held every song ever recorded.

"So, how come the Cubs and the White Sox became

one team?" I asked as we walked down the dirt road toward Bernard's house.

"There was a tornado," he explained. "A big one. It pretty much picked Wrigley Field up off the ground and dumped it into Lake Michigan. A lot of people died that day."

"When was that?" I asked.

"Around 2055," he said. "There have been other changes too. The Florida Marlins are gone. Tampa Bay Rays too. And the Cubs and the Sox weren't the only teams to merge. The Mets and the Yankees became one team in 2066."

"Don't tell me," I said. "They became the New York Mankees."

"How did you know?" he asked.

"Lucky guess."

We approached a field where a man was walking alongside a plow that was being pulled by two horses. Bernard waved to him and told me it was his father.

The future wasn't at all what I expected.

139

Bernard's house was small, and it wasn't in great shape. Some of the shingles were missing from the roof, and there were boards over a few of the windows. I guess his family was poor. Before he pulled open the screen door, Bernard took me aside on the porch, putting a hand on my shoulder.

"I need to tell you something. My parents don't know what you and I can do with baseball cards," he said quietly. "And I'm not going to tell them who you are."

"Why not?" I asked.

"Well, for one thing, I didn't know if the baseball card was going to work," he said. "And I didn't know if I would even be able to find you in Louisville or bring you back here with me. The other thing is, well, my dad is your grandson."

"Yeah, it might be a little weird," I agreed. Grownups sometimes freak out when the world they've become used to is suddenly turned upside down. Kids are more adaptable.

We entered through the kitchen door, and Bernard's mom was in there, slicing carrots at the sink. She smiled. Bernard's dad—my grandson—came in though the other door.

"Mom, Dad," Bernard said, "I just met this kid. His name is Joe."

I couldn't help but stare at my grandson. He was about my dad's age, but he had long hair tied in a ponytail. His face was wrinkled and tanned, as if he spent a lot of time out in the sun. He looked tired.

"Nice to meet you," he said, wiping his hands on a rag before he shook mine. "Joe, huh? My grandfather's name was Joe. I don't remember him, though. He died when I was little."

I gulped.

"Nice to meet you too," I mumbled awkwardly.

"Will you join us for dinner, Joe?" Bernard's mom asked. "We're having spaghetti."

I looked at Bernard, and he nodded.

"Uh, sure," I said. "I guess so."

"You boys be ready in a half hour," she told us. "And wash your hands. You're filthy!"

"C'mon," Bernard said, pulling me through the kitchen, "I want to show you some stuff."

Bernard gave me a tour of the house. What a disappointment! There was no cool futuristic stuff at all. In fact, they didn't even have the stuff I have in *my* house. There was no TV or DVD, no computer, no electric lights or telephones. In the kitchen, there was no microwave, no dishwasher, no toaster. They didn't even have air-conditioning. I was astonished. So much for science fiction.

We went outside and headed for the barn. I didn't want to hurt Bernard's feelings by saying how poor his family seemed to be. But I was genuinely perplexed. Even poor people in my time lived better than this.

"So, what's a typical day like for you?" I asked, trying to be diplomatic.

"Well," he said, "I get up in the morning to feed the

horses and milk the cows. Then I gather the eggs and feed the chickens before school. After school, there are chores, of course. In the early spring, we prepare the field for planting. In the summer, we tend the crops and make hay. Late summer and fall is harvesttime. And in the winter, we do canning—y'know, fruits and vegetables."

The *clop-clop* of hooves interrupted him. Somebody went past the window on a horse.

"I know this isn't what you expected," Bernard continued. "I'm sorry to let you down."

"No, it's fine," I said. "I just thought you would have . . . a lot of cool stuff."

"Yeah, I know," Bernard said with a sigh. "But when you get something new—like a present—you're really happy for an hour, maybe. After that, it doesn't mean much. You start thinking about the next new thing you want to get. And it just goes on and on like that. I decided that stuff doesn't make you happy. *People* make you happy."

I'm sure he was right. There were certain advantages to living this way, I tried to convince myself. Sometimes all the cell phones and emails and text messaging we have to communicate with one another prevents us from ever talking face-to-face. It was peaceful in Bernard's world. With no air-conditioning and no constant hum of machines, you could hear birds chirping. You could hear the silence. It was nice, in a way.

But I wouldn't want to live that way, and I couldn't

help but feel disappointed. This wasn't what the future was supposed to be like. It was almost as if I had traveled to the past instead.

"Can I ask you a personal question?" I asked Bernard.

"Ask away."

"Are you . . . Amish?" I said.

"No," he replied, laughing.

"So does that mean everybody lives like this?"

"Pretty much," he said.

"What happened?" I asked. "It's like everything went backward. And why did you bring me here? It seemed like it was pretty important when you were in my room."

"It is," he said. "It's *very* important. Let's talk in the barn. We'll need some privacy."

20

Bernard's Mission

"I NEED TO SHOW YOU SOMETHING," BERNARD SAID AFTER A long walk to the barn. He closed the door behind us.

A couple of horses looked up when we came in but went right back to eating their hay. In the corner of the barn was an old wooden desk. Bernard opened a drawer and took out a large, rolled-up piece of paper.

At first I thought he was joking.

He slid off the rubber band and unrolled the paper on top of the desk. I leaned over to look at it.

"What happened to Florida?" I asked.

"Oh, it's still there," Bernard said. "But it's submerged."

"That's a joke, right?" I asked.

"No, it's not," he replied seriously.

"Disney World too?" I asked.

"Yeah. Submerged."

"Is that why you said the Marlins and Rays are no longer in the majors?" I asked.

"It's hard to play baseball underwater," Bernard told me.

Wow. That must be thousands of square miles— gone. Houses. Schools. People. When I was little, we took a family trip to Florida. Disney World was one of my first memories.

"What happened?" I asked.

"You'd better sit down, Grandpa," Bernard said, pulling over a chair for each of us. "When you were young, there were these things called polar ice caps."

"I know what polar ice caps are," I said. "I learned about them in school."

"Well, they're not there anymore," Bernard informed me. "The temperature of the ocean kept getting higher and higher until the ice caps melted. It was a long time ago. Anyway, when they melted, the level of the oceans rose. A lot of places got flooded. Most of Florida disappeared. Some islands in the

Pacific disappeared entirely. Millions of people had to move to higher ground. A lot of them died."

"Why did the temperature go up?" I asked.

"You mean you really don't know?" Bernard asked.

"Not exactly," I replied honestly. "Something to do with global warming?"

Bernard sighed as he rolled the map back up and slipped the rubber band around it.

"*'Warming,'*" he said with a snort. "I hate that word. It sounds like a *good* thing. Do you know what carbon dioxide is, Grandpa?"

"Sure," I replied.

"Well," he said, "when you burn oil, coal, or natural gas, it gives off carbon dioxide. It took nature millions of years to create all the fossil fuels that were buried under the surface of the earth. And in about one century, humans burned most of it. Back home in your time, they pump 30 billion tons of carbon dioxide into the air each year."

"And that heats up the atmosphere and the oceans," I said.

"Right," said Bernard. "You asked me about flying cars. Grandpa, we don't even have *regular* cars anymore! The oil ran out *years* ago. World War III was fought over what was left of it."

"There was a world war fought over oil?" I asked.

"In the forties," he said, "before I was born. Grandpa, the reason why you don't see airplanes in the sky here is because we don't have any fuel for them. The reason why you don't see anything made from plastic here is because plastic was made from oil. All those plastic bags, plastic toys, plastic junk . . ."

"I didn't know that plastic is made out of oil," I admitted.

"When the oil was gone," he continued, "they burned coal and wood for fuel. But that gave off carbon dioxide too. All that carbon dioxide was trapped, and the earth's atmosphere eventually heated up to the point that the ice caps melted and the air was virtually unbreathable."

"I know global warming is a problem," I said, "but I didn't know it was that bad."

"Grandpa, do you know what month it is right now?" Bernard asked me.

"July?" I guessed.

"It's December," he told me. "It's 90 degrees out, and it's December. Grandpa, I have never seen snow in my life. Can you imagine how hot it gets here in July?"

"A hundred and ten?" I said.

"Hotter," said Bernard. "You see, everything is connected. Oil was burned, which heated the atmosphere and the oceans. The ice caps melted, which made the sea level rise and cause flooding. Temperatures went up, which forced plants and animals to move, adapt, or become extinct. Food became scarce. Weather became more extreme. We have a tornado here just about every week."

"What happened to downtown Chicago?" I asked.

"Was it destroyed by a tornado?"

"There are *no* cities left, Grandpa!" Bernard exclaimed. "Since your time, people have died by the millions from starvation, disease, and dehydration. We're the lucky ones. My folks knew how to farm. At least we're alive. Grandpa, there's the possibility that we might not make it to the year 2100."

"You mean our family?" I asked.

"I mean the human *race*," Bernard replied seriously. "Civilization is dying, Grandpa. Human life on Earth is *dying*."

"I . . . I didn't know," I began.

"Grandpa, in school they told us that people knew about this problem around the turn of the century. Is that right?"

"Well, yeah," I told him. "It's all over the news. They always talk about going green and saving energy. Stuff like that."

Bernard threw up his hands.

"So why aren't you doing anything about it?" he asked.

"We are," I told him, a little defensively. "I turn off the lights when I leave a room. I take shorter showers. My mom and I reuse our water bottles. We separate our garbage."

"You separate your garbage?" Bernard said with a snort. He shook his head sadly.

"That's not enough?" I asked.

"Not by a long shot," he replied.

"So that's why you brought me here," I said.

"Grandpa," Bernard told me, "we're desperate now. Look around. This is what's going to happen if the people in your time don't do something. The world that you know is going to come to an end."

"What do you want me to do?" I asked.

"It's simple," he replied. "You have to stop burning fossil fuels for energy."

He kept saying *you*. As if I personally was responsible for ruining the world.

"Look, I don't burn *anything*," I said. "I'm just a kid. I can't—"

"Listen," he interrupted. "In my social studies book, it says that in 1961, President Kennedy vowed to send a man to the moon within ten years. And in 1969, we did it. And my book says that in 1939, America started a program called the Manhattan Project to build an atomic bomb before the Nazis could build one. And in 1945, we did it."

"So?"

"Well," Bernard said, "if you can put a man on the moon in less than ten years and build an atomic bomb in six years, how long could it take to stop burning fossil fuels and switch to other kinds of energy?"

"It's not so easy," I told him.

"I know!" Bernard said, raising his voice. "That other stuff wasn't easy either! But it's gotta be done! You've gotta get solar panels up on every rooftop, on every surface where the sun shines! You've gotta get turbines up in every field where the wind blows! There's hydroelectric power, nuclear power, geothermal power, hydrogen fuel cells—all kinds of power. But you've got to go home and convince everybody to stop burning stuff to produce energy. That's why I brought you here."

"A lot of people are gonna be upset when I tell them this," I said.

"Yeah," Bernard said, "well, they're gonna be pretty upset when they have to live like this too."

The horses suddenly became restless in their stalls, stomping the floor and snorting.

A bell rang outside in the distance. Bernard said it meant dinner was ready.

When we opened the barn door, there was a welcome chill in the air. The wind had kicked up, and the sky had turned gray.

"Uh-oh," Bernard said as we stepped outside.

"What's the matter?" I asked. "Do you think your mom will be angry that we didn't wash up?"

"No," he replied. "It looks like a storm is coming. They used to call Chicago the Windy City. They had no idea. We've had to rebuild our house twice, but we can't keep doing it. Come on!"

The distance from the barn to Bernard's house was about the length of a football field. We started running, and about halfway there the rain began coming down. It actually felt good to me after being in the heat, but Bernard had a worried look on his face. Then he suddenly stopped, turned around, and pointed behind us.

I had never seen a tornado before. Well, on the

It was probably a few miles away, but I could smell it.

news, of course. And in that old movie *Twister*. But seeing one in person was an entirely different experience. It was a beautiful thing, in a way. I had to stop and marvel at the huge funnel of swirling blackness. It was probably a few miles away, but I could smell it.

"Mom!" Bernard screamed. "Dad! Everybody! Into the shelter!"

Before Bernard and I reached the house, we changed direction and headed toward the field where we had been playing ball. His parents came running out of the house, holding hands with two little girls.

"Who are they?" I yelled to Bernard.

"My sisters!" he yelled back.

I had to stop for a moment. I had *three* great-grandchildren!

"Hurry, Grandpa!" Bernard screamed, grabbing me.

The wind was whipping all around us now, as the tornado was clearly moving in our direction. Bernard stopped at a spot where there was a large piece of plywood on the ground. He picked it up to reveal a hole big enough for us to fit into.

There was a wooden ladder inside the hole. Bernard ordered me to climb down the ladder. He followed, and then helped the rest of his family.

This was no time for formal introductions and chitchat. Bernard's mother lit candles while his father pulled the plywood back over the top of the hole. The two girls were huddled in the corner, crying.

Even with the candles, it was still very dark in there. I could hear the wind howling above us. The tornado was getting closer.

The shelter was just high enough to stand in, and surprisingly big. There was room in there for shelves full of canned foods, tools, and medical supplies. In fact, there was even a second room. Bernard shoved me in there and closed the door behind us. It was pitch-black until he started turning the crank on an emergency flashlight. The light flickered on.

"I was afraid this might happen," Bernard whispered in my ear. "You've got to go home, right away."

"You mean home to Louisville?" I asked. "Shouldn't I wait until the storm blows over?"

"No," he said. "You've got to go *now*. If something happens to you here and you don't make it home, well . . ."

I knew where he was going. If I got stuck or were to die in 2080, I would never grow up in my own time. I would never have children—or grandchildren.

Bernard would never be born.

"Why don't you come with me!" I asked as I fumbled through my pockets, searching for my pack of new baseball cards. "You don't have to live like this. You can grow up in my time. We'll just say you're my cousin."

"My family is here," Bernard replied. "*You go.*"

"We can come back and get them," I suggested. "There are so many questions I wanted to ask you . . . about me, my family—"

"No time for that!" he said more forcefully. "Hurry up!"

I grabbed something out of my pocket, but it wasn't the pack of cards. It was the hundred-dollar bill and the card Roberto Clemente had given me:

If you have a chance to accomplish something that will make things better for people coming behind you, and you don't do that, you are wasting your time on this earth.

I stuffed them back into my pocket. Finally, I found the baseball cards in my other pocket and ripped off the wrapper. I pulled out a card. The wind was howling louder now. The tornado must have been right over our heads.

"I'm scared, Mommy!" I heard one of the girls whimper from the other room.

"I shouldn't leave you," I told Bernard. "You need my help."

"You can't help us here," he insisted. "You can help us in *your* time."

"What about your parents?" I asked. "What are you gonna tell them? That I just disappeared?"

"I'll think of something," he said, hugging me. "Now get out of here!"

I sat down on the dirt floor and closed my eyes, trying to concentrate on going home. It wasn't easy. It sounded like a jet engine was right above us. I was shivering from the cold dampness of my clothes.

"Do you feel anything?" Bernard asked.

"Not yet," I said.

But as soon as the words were out of my mouth, the faintest tingling sensation brushed my fingertips. It didn't take as long as I thought. The vibrations spread up my arm and across my body. I knew that soon I would be out of there.

"I won't forget you," I told Bernard.

"You know what you need to do," he said.

As my body became lighter, I heard the sound of the plywood being ripped off the storm shelter. There was a crash and some screams.

And then I vanished.

21

Better Late than Never

WELL, I DIDN'T TRIP OVER THE COFFEE TABLE THIS TIME.

I tripped over the footrest of the chair *next* to the coffee table. Then I landed on *top* of the coffee table. Fortunately, it didn't break. Neither did I.

"Joey!" my mother shouted as she came running down the stairs. "Where *were* you?"

"I was in Chicago, Mom! In 2080! You won't believe—"

"You had me worried sick!" my mother complained. "I was fast asleep, and I heard you in your room saying something about Grandpa. I figured you were having a dream; but when I went in there to see if you were okay, you were gone. I was just about to call the police. Don't scare me like that!"

"I'm sorry, Mom," I said. "But listen, this is important. We need to change everything. We need to get a smaller car that gets better gas mileage. We have to use less energy. We have to stop burning fossil fuels."

"What? Are you crazy?" she said. "Joey, I'm late for work. Coach Valentini keeps calling. He's really mad. Your game started almost an *hour* ago. I can give you a ride over to the field, but we have to leave right away."

I dashed upstairs to change into my uniform. When I took off my jeans, I remembered the hundred-dollar bill in my pocket. That money really shouldn't be lying around. It should be in a safe place. But there was no time to go to the bank now. I stuffed the bill in the pocket of my baseball pants for the time being.

Mom was in the car with the engine running when I came dashing out the front door with my equipment bag. She took a shortcut to Dunn Field, running a couple of stop signs along the way. By the time I jumped out of the car, the scoreboard said it was the bottom of the sixth inning. We were losing, 6-5. Mom asked me to find a ride home after the game and drove off to work.

"Where in the heck have you *been*?" Flip hollered when I ran over to the dugout.

"It's a long story," I said.

"Save it," Flip told me. "Grab a bat. You're on deck."

Usually when guys show up late, Flip makes them sit on the bench as punishment. He must have been really desperate if he was putting me in the game. As

I took a bat out of the rack, I looked around, trying to size up the situation. Brian Wenzel was on first base, and Danny Cretney was on second. Jack Naughton was up. There was a lefty on the mound. The scoreboard said there was one out.

If Jack hit a double or better, I realized, both runners would score and the game would be over. I wouldn't even come to bat.

That was fine with me. The way I had been hitting lately, the best thing I could do for the team would be to stay as far away from a batter's box as possible.

"C'mon, Jack!" I shouted. "Win it for us right now!"

Jack took a couple of pitches, one of them a strike and the other one in the dirt. On the next pitch, he hit an easy grounder toward second.

Everybody on our bench groaned. It was a perfect double play ball. All the second baseman had to do was field the grounder cleanly and flip it to the shortstop, who would throw to first. Game over. We lose. Part of me was actually hoping that would happen, because I really did not want to come to bat.

But it didn't happen that way. The second baseman bobbled the grounder for a moment. He didn't have time to make a play at second, so he scrambled to pick up the ball and barely threw out Luke at first.

Brian and Danny advanced to second and third on the play. Two outs now.

"Stosh!" Flip shouted. "Yer up!"

The metal bat felt light in my hands compared to the wooden one I'd used in 2080. I took a few practice swings and walked slowly to the plate. Why did I always get myself into these situations? A hit would drive in the two runs and win the game. An out would lose it. And I was in the worst batting slump of my life.

"Wait for a good one, Stosh!" Flip yelled, clapping his hands.

"Make him throw strikes, Stosh!" hollered Brian.

I have always been a patient hitter. I take pride in the fact that I have a good sense of the strike zone and refuse to swing at pitches that aren't over the plate. But lately, that strategy wasn't working. I needed to try something different.

I tried to think back and recall what Roberto Clemente had told me about getting out of a batting slump. I remembered the question he'd asked me: "Who do you think has more chances to hit the ball: a batter who takes three swings—or a batter who takes one swing?"

That had stuck with me. Of course, the batter who takes three swings has the better chance of hitting the ball.

The heck with it, I decided. I'm just going to swing at everything. I don't care if the ball is behind my head. I'm going to take a whack at it. What did I have to lose?

The pitcher looked in for the sign, wound up, and let fly. The pitch was a little high, but I went for it anyway. Missed it. Strike one.

"Whaddaya swingin' at, Stosh?" Flip yelled. "That was over yer head!"

I didn't care. There was something liberating about going up there and knowing I was going to rip at the pitch no matter what. If you don't have to think so hard about whether or not you should swing, you can put more energy and concentration into the swing itself. It felt good to take a wild cut for a change.

I dug in. The pitcher peeked at the runners on second and third, and then wheeled and delivered.

It was outside. I reached out and swung anyway. The ball ticked off the end of my bat. At least I got a piece of it.

"Stosh, are you outta yer mind?" Flip yelled. "That pitch was in Indiana! Now yer down two strikes!"

I didn't care if I was down *ten* strikes. I was going to keep taking my cuts. If that strategy was good enough for Roberto Clemente, it was good enough for me.

I fouled off the next three pitches. One of them might have been a strike. Maybe not.

"Fuhgetuhboutit," Flip said, throwing his hands up.

The pitcher must have been getting tired of toying with me. Or maybe he was just getting tired. But the next pitch was over the heart of the plate. I slashed at it, and the ball jumped off my bat with a nice *ping*. The shortstop leaped for it, but it was a foot or two above his glove.

"Go! Go! Go!" everybody was yelling.

Danny scored easily from third; and when the ball skipped between the two outfielders and went all the way to the wall, Brian trotted home too. That was the winning run.

Everybody mobbed me when I got back to the bench. Flip put me in a headlock and told me I was a lucky son of a gun. He may have been right. But I broke out of my slump, we won the game, and that was all that mattered.

I was packing up my stuff on the bench when Tommy Rose suddenly said, "Oh no, not again."

I turned around and saw those Girl Scouts parading through the bleachers with their signs and cans.

"SAVE THE POLAR BEARS!" they chanted. "SAVE THE POLAR BEARS!"

I stood and watched them walk around asking people to donate money. Me and the guys had always made fun of those girls doing their good deeds. Polar bears! The only polar bear I'd ever seen in my whole life was on TV. It had all seemed so silly.

But after my experience in 2080, it didn't feel silly anymore. These girls didn't have to be spending their time raising money to save polar bears. They could have been out with their friends, having fun or whatever. But they really cared about something. And it wasn't just that they cared. Anybody can *care*. They were *doing* something. I had to admire them for that.

I thought about all the places I had been the last couple of days. Woodstock. Cincinnati. Chicago. And I remembered the hundred-dollar bill in my pocket. I reached in to make sure it was still there.

It was.

22

A Quick Trip

I THOUGHT REALLY SERIOUSLY ABOUT DONATING THE hundred-dollar bill to the Girl Scouts. That would have blown everybody's minds. But then I came up with another idea.

"Flip!" I yelled. "Can I talk to you for a sec?"

He was packing up his car and getting ready to go home. Flip drives a big old Cadillac with tail fins, one of the few left on the road. To some people, it would be an antique. To Flip, it's just his car.

"What can I do ya for, Stosh?" he said as I jogged over.

"Do you have any baseball cards with you?"

"Does a squirrel have nuts?" he replied. "Whaddaya need?"

Flip is probably the only guy in the world who drives around with a trunk full of baseball cards. He popped open the trunk and I peered inside. There must have been thousands of cards in there, stuffed haphazardly into shoe boxes.

"Do you have one from 1972?" I asked.

"Anybody in particular?" Flip asked. "I got Johnny Bench . . . Lou Brock . . . Nolan Ryan . . . Harmon Killebrew . . ."

"It doesn't matter," I told him. "Any 1972 card will do. Oh, and I need a new card too."

Flip rooted around back there until he found what I wanted. Then he slipped the two cards into plastic sleeves and handed them to me.

"What are you cookin' up *now,* Stosh?" he said, looking at me with a crooked grin.

"Just give me ten minutes," I told him. "I'll be right back."

"You *are* crazy," Flip said, shaking his head.

I opened the passenger door of Flip's car and slid inside. I stuck the new card into my back pocket and slipped the 1972 card out of its sleeve. Then I closed my eyes and concentrated.

Wait! There was something else I needed.

In the beverage holder between the front seats, there were a couple of quarters and dimes that Flip uses to pay tolls. I scooped them up and put them in my pocket, making a mental note to pay Flip back. Then I closed my eyes again.

I didn't care where I landed. Just as long as it was 1972.

It didn't take long. Soon the tingling sensation arrived, and then the feeling of lightness. I was fading away . . . and fading away . . . and fading away . . .

And I was gone.

When I opened my eyes, I was sitting on a bench in a bus stop next to a lady with a shopping bag. There were some stores across the street. The lady looked up from the book she had been reading and smiled at me.

"Excuse me, ma'am," I asked. "Is there a post office around here?"

She looked puzzled and shrugged her shoulders. *"No hablo Ingles,"* she said.

Just my luck. She didn't speak English.

Wait! It was okay. This one I could handle.

"¿Donde esta el correo?" I asked.

She smiled and pointed down the street. I told her *mucho gracias* and ran off.

The sign on the building said UNITED STATES POST OFFICE—CLAYTON, MISSOURI. I rushed inside. This was going to be a long shot, I knew, but I had to give it a try.

There was nobody waiting in line, so I went right up to the counter. A little sign said TODAY'S DATE IS OCTOBER 27, 1972.

"I'd like to buy one envelope, please," I said to the lady behind the counter. I fished the hundred-dollar bill out of my pocket and slipped it into the envelope she gave me.

"That's a lot of money to be sending through the mail," the lady told me. "Do you want insurance?"

"No, thank you," I said as I licked the envelope and sealed it. There was a pen on the counter that was attached to a little chain. I wrote this neatly on the outside of the envelope:

Señorita Molina
San Jorge Children's Hospital
San Juan, Puerto Rico

"Do you know the street address?" the lady asked.

I shook my head.

"Well, I think it will still get there," she said.

"I hope so," I told her. "It's very important."

She put the envelope on a small scale to weigh it.

"That will be ten cents, please," she said. "Two for the envelope and eight for the postage."

"Are you serious?" I asked.

"I'm afraid so," she replied. "The rates went up last year."

"No, I mean, you can send a letter all the way to Puerto Rico for just eight cents?"

"Would you like to pay more?" she asked with a smile.

I gave her a dime and she promised to take special care to make sure my envelope made it to Puerto Rico.

"Do you need a receipt?" she asked.

"No thanks."

A chair was off to the side, behind a wall and near

the post office boxes. There were no customers around. It was quiet, and private. I sat down and pulled out the new baseball card Flip had loaned me.

Home, I thought. I just want to go home. Get something to eat. Go to sleep.

I might have dozed off for a minute or two. The sound of approaching footsteps woke me up—and so did the feeling of a tingling sensation in my fingertips. Then there was the voice of the post office lady who'd helped me at the window.

"Are you okay, young man?" she asked.

"Yes," I said, my eyes still shut. "I'm just . . . a little dizzy."

The vibrations were getting stronger, moving up my arm and across my body.

"Do you need a doctor?"

"No," I whispered. "I'm fine. I'll be gone in a few seconds."

My whole body was vibrating. I wouldn't have been able to stop it if I wanted to.

"You forgot to put a return address on your envelope," she informed me. "I can do it for you. Where do you live?"

"Where do I live?" I whispered. "I live . . . in the future."

And then I faded away.

When I opened my eyes, I was sitting in the passenger seat of Flip's car again. He was sitting next to me reading *Sports Illustrated*. He was startled when I suddenly appeared.

"Thanks, Flip," I said, shaking my head to clear it. "You can have those cards back."

"Where were you, Stosh?" Flip asked.

"In Missouri, in 1972."

"What the heck were you doin' there?"

"The usual," I told him. "Trying to save somebody's life."

"You are one crazy kid, Stosh. You know that?"

"I guess I am."

"As long as you're sittin' here, you need a ride home?" asked Flip.

"Yeah," I said. "It's been a rough couple of days."

23

Extra Credit

I HATE MONDAYS. ESPECIALLY MONDAYS LIKE THIS MONDAY, when we get our report cards. Most schools send out report cards by mail, so you don't see the bad news until you get home. At my school, they hand them out first thing in the morning, during homeroom. That way you have the whole day to figure out how you're going to explain things to your parents.

"... Morrisey ... Peters ... Ralston ..."

My homeroom teacher, Mr. Meyer, was calling out our names in alphabetical order.

"... Soriano ... Stoshack ..."

I marched up to the front of the class, and Mr. Meyer handed me my envelope. Why do they even bother putting them in envelopes? I started ripping it open before I got back to my seat.

What?!

I had to look at it twice. Maybe the name was

wrong and they gave me somebody else's report card by mistake, I figured. No, that's me. Maybe somebody was goofing on me and they changed my grade.

STUDENT REPORT CARD Stoshack, Joseph							

Homeroom: Mr. Meyer
Advisor: Ms. Judith Dorfman
Grade: 7

		Sem 1		Sem 2		
		1	2	3	4	YR
Absent		3				
Tardy		0				

Class	Semester 1			Semester 2			Final Grade	Credit Earned	Comment
	1	2	Mid Exam	3	4	Final Exam			
Language Arts	89								
Social Studies	91								
Spanish	95								*nice work!*
Physical Education	100								
Mathematics	93								
Health	100								

I got an A in Spanish!

Nope, there were no signs of tampering.

I, Joe Stoshack, aced Spanish!

Still, it had to be a mistake, I figured. Just a few days ago I got that progress report saying I was flunking Spanish. How could I bring my grade up to an A so fast?

For once, I was glad I had Spanish first period on Mondays. The bell rang, and everybody bolted out of homeroom like it was the Olympics or something. We only have three minutes between classes, and you get detention if you're one second late.

I got to Señorita Molina's room before any of the other kids. There was a candle burning on her desk, as usual, and she was standing at the whiteboard.

Wait a minute.

Standing?!

I stopped in the doorway. Where was her wheel-chair? Not only was Señorita Molina standing on her own two feet, but the whiteboard was three feet higher than it used to be. For a moment, I thought I had walked into the wrong class.

"Buenos dias, Tito," Señorita Molina said. "Did you do anything interesting over the weekend?"

Well, yeah! It looked like I changed Señorita Molina's whole life over the weekend! But at first I really couldn't comprehend that it was true.

"Señorita, where is your wheelchair?" I asked her.

"Wheelchair?" she said. "What wheelchair?"

"You know," I said, "the one you sit in all the time?"

A couple of kids who came in behind me started giggling.

"Stoshack *es loco,*" somebody said.

"Don't you remember?" I said to Señorita Molina. "When you were very young, you had an infection in your spine and you needed antibiotics, but your family didn't have the money and . . ."

"I really don't know what you're talking about, Tito," Señorita Molina said. "Take your seat, please."

"But you told me . . ."

"Estas bien?" she said, putting her hand on my forehead just like my mother does when she thinks

I have a fever. "Do you need to go see the nurse, Tito?"

"Uh, no."

I just stood there for a minute, dazed. Everybody was laughing at me, but I didn't care.

I did it!

Señorita Molina must have received the envelope I'd mailed to her in 1972. Her parents used the hundred dollars to buy the antibiotics she needed. It cured her infection, and she didn't need the wheelchair!

She has no memory that it even happened, I realized. She was so young. The medicine took care of the infection, and it wasn't a significant event in her life. She has no idea I was responsible.

Maybe I didn't save Roberto Clemente's life, but I *did* change history.

"Is there anything else, Tito?" Señorita Molina asked. "We need to start class now."

"Oh, I just wanted to thank you for the A you gave me on my report card," I said.

"Don't thank me," she said. "It was your extra credit project. Very imaginative."

Extra credit project? I didn't remember doing any extra credit project.

Confused, I went to my seat. I was still thinking about what had just happened.

Just to make sure I wasn't completely out of my mind, I looked up at Señorita Molina again.

And I can't be completely sure, but I think she threw me a wink.

Facts and Fictions

Everything in this book is true, except for the stuff I made up. It's only fair to tell you which is which.

It is definitely true that Roberto Clemente was one of baseball's greatest players. But more importantly, he was one of baseball's greatest *people*. After a short lifetime filled with humanitarian efforts, on New Year's Eve 1972 he died in a plane crash while attempting to deliver food and medicine to victims of an earthquake in Nicaragua. His body was never found.

Major League Baseball's highest honor for community service is the Roberto Clemente Man of the Year Award, which is given each year to a player who combines outstanding skills on the field with devoted work in the community.

There are at least forty schools called Roberto Clemente School worldwide. Two hundred parks and baseball fields have been named in his memory, as well as two hospitals in Puerto Rico.

Clemente loved working with children, and in 1959 he first dreamed of building a sports city where poor kids could learn not just how to play, but also how to be good citizens. That dream was finally realized when Roberto's wife, Vera, and their sons opened Roberto Clemente Sports City in Carolina, Puerto Rico, the town where he grew up. It has turned out stars such as Ivan Rodriguez, Benito Santiago, Ruben Sierra, and Roberto and Sandy Alomar Jr.

Clemente was the first Hispanic player to win a batting title and also the first to be voted into the Baseball Hall of Fame. Much like Jackie Robinson a generation earlier, Roberto Clemente paved the way and inspired hundreds of Latin American players. Today, about a quarter of all major-league players are

Latino. Some of them, such as Jose Guillen, Ruben Sierra, and Sammy Sosa, wore number 21 in honor of Roberto Clemente.

Roberto was also well-known for his physical ailments. It is true that he needed to have his neck "booped" to move the disks back into place. He was also an amateur chiropractor and would use his healing touch to help teammates and sometimes strangers. And he loved fruit milk shakes.

Most of the information about Roberto came from David Maraniss's biography *Clemente: The Passion and Grace of Baseball's Last Hero.* I also got a lot of good material from *Roberto Clemente: The Great One,* by Bruce Markusen.

I wish I was there, but I did not attend the Woodstock Festival in 1969. With the help of books and videos, I tried to capture the look and feel of the event. Peter, Wendy, and Sunrise are fictional characters, but lots of hippies drove Volkswagen vans to and from Woodstock. Other fictional characters in this story include Stosh, his parents, Bernard and his family, Flip, and Señorita Molina.

The Pittsburgh Pirates did play at Crosley Field in Cincinnati on the night Woodstock ended, but Bob Moose was not the pitcher, and the play-by-play described here is not identical to the actual game. Clemente's heroics described in that game were actually condensed from plays he made over the course of his career. Crosley Field was torn down in 1972. And the Mets did make a dramatic come-from-behind charge in 1969, winning 38 of their last 49 games—and the World Series.

Since the beginning of time, people have been trying to predict the future, and usually failing. We will probably *never* have flying cars or personal jet packs.

Nobody today knows what life will be like in the year 2080. But many scientists believe that unless we stop burning fossil fuels and switch to solar, wind, and other clean sources of energy, we are heading toward an environmental disaster. You can do something about it. If you want your great-grandchildren to have a different life than Joe Stoshack's great-grandson, here are some websites I urge you to visit:

EPA Climate Change Kids Site
(www.epa.gov/globalwarming/kids) Learn about the greenhouse effect, how humans change the climate, and what we can do about it.

What's Up with the Weather?
(www.pbs.org/wgbh/warming) This PBS site helps you find out how much fossil fuel you use.

The Green Squad (www.nrdc.org/greensquad) Kids taking action to make greener, healthier schools.

Environmental Kids Club (www.epa.gov/kids) A

club for kids interested in learning more about the environment and in getting involved in environmental activities.

Tree Musketeers (www.treemusketeers.org) An organization dedicated to empowering young people to lead environmental improvement movements.

It's Getting Hot In Here
(http://itsgettinghotinhere.org) A growing movement of student and youth leaders who aim to stop global warming and to build a more just and sustainable future.

Natural Resources Defense Council
(www.nrdc.org) They work to protect the planet—its people, plants, and animals—and to help create a new way of life for humankind, without fouling or depleting the resources that support all life on Earth.

Sierra Club (www.sierraclub.org) This is America's oldest, largest, and most influential environmental organization. More than a million members work to protect the planet.

Greenpeace (www.greenpeaceusa.org) Since 1971, they have been fighting to protect the environment through education and activism.

Stop Global Warming
(www.stopglobalwarming.org) A movement to demand that our leaders freeze and reduce carbon dioxide emissions.

As you go about helping others, remember Roberto Clemente's words: *"If you have a chance to accomplish something that will make things better for people coming behind you, and you don't do that, you are wasting your time on this earth."*

Roberto Clemente's Career Statistics

Year	Team	Games	At Bats	Hits	Doubles	Triples	Home Runs	Runs Batted In	Batting Average
1954	Montreal	87	148	38	5	3	2	12	.257
1955	Pittsburgh	124	474	121	23	11	5	47	.255
1956	Pittsburgh	147	543	169	30	7	7	60	.311
1957	Pittsburgh	111	451	114	17	7	4	30	.253
1958	Pittsburgh	140	519	150	24	10	6	50	.289
1959	Pittsburgh	105	432	128	17	7	4	50	.296
1960	Pittsburgh	144	570	179	22	6	16	94	.314
1961	Pittsburgh	146	572	201	30	10	23	89	.351
1962	Pittsburgh	144	538	168	28	9	10	74	.312
1963	Pittsburgh	152	600	192	23	8	17	76	.320
1964	Pittsburgh	155	622	211	40	7	12	87	.339
1965	Pittsburgh	152	589	194	21	14	10	65	.329
1966	Pittsburgh	154	638	202	31	11	29	119	.317
1967	Pittsburgh	147	585	209	26	10	23	110	.357
1968	Pittsburgh	132	502	146	18	12	18	57	.291
1969	Pittsburgh	138	507	175	20	12	19	91	.345
1970	Pittsburgh	108	412	145	22	10	14	60	.352
1971	Pittsburgh	132	522	178	29	8	13	86	.341
1972	Pittsburgh	102	378	118	19	7	10	60	.312
Total		2433	9454	3000	440	166	240	1305	.317

National League Batting Champion: 1961, 1964, 1965, 1967
National League Most Valuable Player: 1966
World Series Most Valuable Player: 1971
National League Outfield Assist Leader: 1958 (22), 1960 (19), 1961 (27), 1966 (17), 1967 (17)
National League All-Star: 1960-67, 1969-71
Gold Glove: 1961-72

Permissions

This author would like to acknowledge the following for use of photographs: Pittsburgh Pirates, 25, 78, 81, 84. The Topps Company, Inc., 32. National Baseball Hall of Fame Library, Cooperstown, NY, 95, 173. Nina Wallace, 127, 144, 169. Library of Congress, 139, 151.

About the Author

This is Dan Gutman's tenth baseball card adventure. If you like it, check out *Honus & Me, Jackie & Me, Babe & Me, Shoeless Joe & Me, Mickey & Me, Abner & Me, Satch & Me, Jim & Me*, and *Ray & Me*. Dan (pictured here at age 12) is also the author of *The Kid Who Ran for President, The Homework Machine, The Million Dollar Shot, Johnny Hangtime*, and the My Weird School series. You can find out more about Dan and his books at www.dangutman.com.